BLUEGRASS BOUNTY

The most wanted gunman and outlaw this side of the Rockies, Jude Lovell, is about to hang in the town of Saracen. The crowds flock to be at the event of the century. But Marshal Brand is deeply suspicious. Why are there so many of Lovell's gang gathered in the town? Have they come to mourn, or to stage a daring rescue? When the awful truth dawns it wreaks a devastating toll of death and destruction.

*Books by Jack Reason
in the Linford Western Library:*

ROUGHSHOD
TORN LEATHER
DIRT TRAIL DRIFTER
HIGH MILE RIDER
RIVERBEND RANSOM
BLADE LAW

JACK REASON

BLUEGRASS BOUNTY

Complete and Unabridged

LINFORD
Leicester

First published in Great Britain in 2007 by
Robert Hale Limited
London

First Linford Edition
published 2008
by arrangement with
Robert Hale Limited
London

British Library CIP Data

Reason, Jack
  Bluegrass bounty.—Large print ed.—
Linford western library
1. Western stories
2. Large type books
I. Title
823.9′14 [F]

ISBN 978–1–84782–434–9

This one for J. L. B.

1

The news travelled faster than the high winds could carry it. The outlaw, robber, notorious gunslinger, Jude Lovell, had been taken, captured alive by a couple of fast-thinking, trigger-smart bounty hunters in the foothills of the Bigbones.

And not only taken alive, but unscathed; not so much as a mark on the fellow saving where others had tried before and failed. This was Jude Lovell in mint condition, as fit as he would ever be for a hanging that would be celebrated through the length and breadth of the territory, in every town, every homestead, every nook and gopher cranny; a celebration the likes of which had never been seen before. It would be a historic occasion, as close as made no odds to a festival.

Why, there was serious talk in important civic places of declaring the hanging day a public holiday, one that would be marked down the years and into posterity as the day folk were free once again of threat and tyranny, death and destruction at the whim of a gunman, when men could sleep safe at night alongside their wives and have no fears for the fate of their daughters; when the presidents of banks and stage-line companies could rest easy, secure in the knowledge they would not be the next on the Lovell hit list.

And the fast growing companies back East breathed a sigh of their own relief at the thought that Jude Lovell and his boys would not be a plague on their efforts in the big — and expensive — push West. Even the riverboat skippers blew a blast of joy. There would be partying long into the night and for many nights to come.

As news of the capture spread and gained momentum in the telling, so the details of just what had happened in the Bigbones mountain range began to emerge — real or imaginatively embellished no one quite knew.

Some early versions of the taking had it that the bounty hunters were professionals out of Texas. Later, the hunters were variously hailed to be from Oregon, Michigan, as far west as Colorado and way beyond the Rockies. A particular version claimed the hunters to be no less than the famous McGill brothers out of Montana. They had made a whole way of life, and a considerable fortune, out of bringing the wanted to justice and claiming the reward. The brothers had quickly denied any involvement.

The only real-life witness to the capture had been long-time gold panner, Scrapes Tuppence, who had subsequently reported his experience to a passing wagon-line headed for the town of Saracen to replenish supplies.

Scrapes had told of how he had seen 'close up and with my own two eyes, God save my soul, no less than Jude Lovell roped — *roped*, I tell you — to his mount trailed by a couple of mean-eyed, slant-lipped sonsofbitches. Bounty guns if ever I saw 'em, and Lovell ridin' meek as a lamb to wherever them hunters planned on takin' him. Saracen like as not.'

Encouraged, if not exactly prompted, Scrapes said he was sure as he was of his own sanity that Lovell had been taken the night before.

'I don't sleep none too deep these nights,' he had explained. 'I see most things, hear most things, and that night I was aware of them bounty boys closin' in on somethin' or somebody. Lovell would have been sleepin' come that dark night with a moon scuddin' through cloud and wouldn't have seen, much less heard, them fellas creepin' up on him like mountain lions. Yessir, they knew their trade sure enough: soft as watchin' mice, keen as rats to fresh food, and armed to the hilt. Took him easy as peelin' apples. Lovell would never have known 'til he opened his eyes. Never stood a chance. And now they'll bring him in large as life, into Saracen and pocket that thousand dollars sittin' on the scumbag's head. Good luck to 'em, and Amen to that . . . '

And so as the euphoria of the capture continued apace across the territory and Saracen prepared to receive its most famous — and infamous — visitor, men far and wide took to the trail to stand witness in their own lifetime to the only show there would ever be in any town: the hanging of Jude Lovell.

Among those men making the long journey was territorial marshal Lyle Brand, attending Saracen in his official capacity as witness to the hanging once the circuit judge had heard the necessary representations, pronounced judgment and settled the date of the hanging.

This would be the marshal's last official duty before he retired after more than thirty years upholding the law and took himself off to that cabin on the river where he planned to fish and sleep, take a measure or two, then fish some more and sleep some more and do it all over again the next day.

Even so, he was a mite troubled, as he finally cleared the sticky, dust-choking rigours of the Bigbones range and dropped gratefully to the cooler breezes and easier going of the bluegrass plains and the last miles to Saracen.

Why, he was wondering, had a man like Jude Lovell been alone in the mountains?

2

Saracen fell to a frenzy. News of the capture and bringing in of Jude Lovell transformed an otherwise thriving and increasingly prosperous settlement into an almost overnight teeming bustle of anticipation and confusion.

Folk arrived — on foot, on horseback, in wagons — by the score from sun-up to sunset. They came from the territory's most northern reaches; from the burned sands of the deepest south, the remote west, the generally more populated eastern counties — each and everyone of them intent and determined to witness the hanging of the man they had lived a lifetime hating. Justice was about to be done: Jude Lovell was going to the gallows. And damnation to his soul!

The importance of the occasion of the hanging would be not so much in seeing Lovell dance at the end of the rope as in being there — right there in the very street where it happened. Witness to the death of Jude Lovell would be a record for history to which men would look back and see the very core of their values of freedom and decency upheld.

Yessir — and Saracen had the privilege of staging it!

Not every one took such a high moral ground. Jim Squire at the mercantile saw profit and a fast return on the stock he was holding almost treble. Folk needed all manner of goods once arrived in town. Jim Squire was there, exclusively, to provide them. That was good business. That was profitability.

Big dollar takings were almost paining the eyes of Charlton Folde, sole proprietor and mine host at the Garter Saloon, where liquor sales were soaring. Meal places were at a premium, rooms non-existent, and beds, save those shared on a strict time limit basis with bar girls, 'unavailable for the foreseeable future'.

The only future Folde could see was shod with money, the largest amounts he had ever seen and would like as not never see again.

Saracen's only bank, the County and Territories, under the direct ownership of Milton Boyd, suffered a similar fate of sudden abundant riches as the visitors arrived. It grew, again overnight, from solvency and acceptable profitability — skimmed off the backs of those who could, by Boyd's accounting, afford it — to a boom banking business worth hundreds of thousands. And growing by the hour. Milton Boyd, in fact, was rated the only man in town with a headache most men would beg for.

Much the same went for the town's two rooming-houses — long booked to the rafters — and the livery, where Jess Morden was doing his best to accommodate and feed more horses than was decent. He had recruited help where he could find it. Lately Poole at the barbers had clipped enough hair to fill his outback shack, and poured enough baths to 'float a half of the town clean through to the border'. After-lotion had risen in price to three dollars a shot — when available. All business strictly cash only.

For Scrapes Tuppence — 'Don't forget, folks, I seen it first. I was there. Saw it for myself' — it had been a case of getting himself into town as fast as possible in order to live off his lucky exposure to the capture of Lovell for as long as he could and while ever folk were ready to listen.

He had no shortage of audiences more than willing to encourage him with quality whiskey and supplies of food to tell his story. Time and time and time again until 'you'd be thinkin' Scrapes took the fella himself!' as one town man was heard to remark. But while ever the audiences gathered and 'paid' their way, Scrapes was happy to perform. For once in his life he had hit a boom time.

But it was all far from an easy-going ride to boom and profit for Sheriff Brad

McConnell and his two deputies. For them, a town teeming with excited sightseers intent on having themselves one almighty hoedown in celebration of the capture of Jude Lovell was little short of a nightmare.

It was bad enough trying to keep a check on the characters arriving — not all were upright and law abiding — and marking out the unsavoury types here to make a fast dollar wherever they could see the chance, there was a whole rattlebag of petty disputes, arguments and blatant exploitations to sort out and settle. Anything, the sheriff reckoned, from standing as arbiter on a disputed claim to who was first for the last bed, to rescuing an unfortunate bar girl from the clutches of an over-excited, drink-sodden loony who had probably not seen civilization in a year or more.

'Enough to try a man's patience to the raw,' he had told his deputies. 'The sooner Marshal Brand is here and that stage carryin' Circuit Judge Whinnie arrives the better. Let's just cut to the darned hangin' and be done with it. Hell — though I wouldn't say it outside the walls of my own office — I could almost wish Lovell was still free!'

A day later the man himself, flanked by his two captors, rode into a silent, unmoving, near dumbstruck reception crowding the main street and swarming like flies for a vantage point across every roof and frontage where a foot or handhold might be gained.

They were seeing Jude Lovell in the flesh, real and alive; the man of legend, the fastest gun this side of any place known to man; the smartest thinker who could outwit a lion and come up from behind to pull its tail! A man whom others had died for and willingly so; whom women had loved and feared in equal measure; who some said would never die, *could* never die, not while he had eyes to see and hands to reach for a gun. And now he was here, within minutes of being behind bars.

Who would have thought it possible?

3

It was Sheriff McConnell's decision to let the bounty hunters address themselves in person to the thronging mass crowding the street outside his office.

'Lovell ain't my first headache right now, boys,' he had said, facing the two men from behind his desk. 'He's secure 'til others decide the procedure. No, it's that lot out there. I'd be real obliged to you both if you'd go tell 'em in your own words just how you came to make this remarkable — and I might say, historic — capture. Tell it to 'em just as it was. Ain't no cause for frills. Give 'em the hard spit and dirt of it, and that, hopefully, should satisfy their curiosity for a while, least-ways 'til we get to the hangin'.'

McConnell poured two generous measures of whiskey from the bottle he kept locked in his private cupboard and invited the men to drink. 'Might as well get started, eh? You boys'll be drinkin' your way through town in a short whiles. But take my advice: you got a big pay day comin' up once territorial Marshal Brand and Circuit Judge Whinnie get here in a couple of days' time to verify matters. With the money comin' your way, you'll be able to buy your own bar, not to mention half the women in town! So take your time, eh? You've done the hard bit, fellas. You just leave Jude Lovell to me, go tell your story, then enjoy yourselves. Saracen awaits you!'

* * *

'They don't look like bounty hunters,' said a youth craning for a better view as the sheriff's door opened and a beaming, square-shouldered McConnell led the two men on to the boardwalk.

'What's a bounty hunter look like, anyhow?' asked a man at the youth's side.

'I don't know for sure,' said the youth, still craning, 'but I'd figure kinda mean and hungry, like he'd kill with bare hands for a decent meal.'

'They'll have enough to eat their way from here to St Louis with the dollars hittin' their pockets soon,' quipped a third man, raising himself on tiptoes.

'Let's hear 'em, shall we?' silenced an old-timer impatiently.

'Right folks,' said McConnell, raising his arms for attention. 'Now I know you ain't here to hear me.'

'Too right we ain't!' shouted a voice from the back.

'Or to look at you,' added his partner to the general amusement of the crowd.

McConnell smiled and continued, 'You've heard Scrapes Tuppence's eye-witness account of the takin' of Jude Lovell more than once — and doubtless will again. But right now, right here in Saracen, we have the two fellas who did the actual capturin' of the man now safely locked in a cell. So, your full attention, please, for, on my left, Chet

15

Freeman, and on my right, Lud Smith.'

A spontaneous round of applause broke out. Some men cheered. Some whistled. A bar girl waved a garter from a bedroom window. Jim Squire checked a list of the goods fast selling out at the store. Milton Boyd temporarily locked and bolted the bank until the partying, as he saw it, was over and normal business resumed. Charlton Folde fingered a fat roll of dollars before stuffing it tightly into a pocket of his pants. Lately Poole scuffed ankle-deep hair and stubble aside. The livery forge billowed thick grey smoke.

'We'd been trailin' close on Lovell's heels for close on a week,' began Freeman, stepping forward, striking an already confident pose as he hooked his thumbs into his belt and twitched a thigh muscle just enough to shift the holstered Colt on his right leg into threat. 'A good deal before that, in fact; pickin' up tracks, losin' 'em, findin' 'em again. But we always knew we had Lovell within reach.'

'How? How come you knew that?' snapped a voice from the crowd.

Freeman sneered. 'Darn it, we could smell him!'

The street buzzed. Men nodded, murmured, jostled an elbow into ribs. Voices called, 'Who wouldn't smell the rat, eh? Who wouldn't? You can always smell a rat.'

'All his stinkin' past. That's what you were smellin'!'

'Wearin' the blood of his killin's like a shirt!'

'All them decent folk, and women too.'

'Yeah, women and young gals whenever he had a fancy.'

'No regard to age neither.'

'And some say how he once took a whole wagonload of 'em, and not one of 'em lived. Not one.'

'Goddamn it, if it'd been me out there trailin' on his miserable butt I'd have shot the louse there and then. Shot him point blank! Then cut his throat and skinned him!'

The crowd rose in a chorus of

shouts, then applause; fists waved, feet stamped. The bar girl at the window threw the garter to the crowd. Three more followed. An elderly lady huffed and drew her husband into shadow. A young man kissed a young girl and blushed violently.

Sheriff McConnell raised his arms again and pleaded for quiet. 'Give the fellas a chance here,' he shouted above the babble of voices. 'We ain't nowhere near hearin' the full story.'

'So let's hear it,' piped a voice.

Freeman relaxed, smirked, glanced at the bar girls at the windows, waved and winked.

Lud Smith stepped to his partner's side. 'We figured on dusk bein' the right time to take him, just when he was gettin' dozy; when the long, hot day up there in them mountains takes a miserable toll of the best of us.'

The crowd nodded, but stayed silent.

Freeman took up the account. 'Lud here skirted through deep rock and went up ahead of me in readiness for

Lovell settlin'. Minute he did, we'd close in: one behind, one up front.'

'And he didn't never hear a thing of you, that what you're sayin'?' clipped the old-timer at the front of the crowd. 'He must've been a whole sight ridin' easy by my reckonin'.'

'He was,' hastened Smith almost before the old man had drawn breath. 'Real relaxed . . . like he was . . . well, kinda into thinkin' somethin' through . . . reckonin' and, hell, who knows with a scumbag like that?'

'Anyhow,' added Freeman quickly, 'we closed in real slow, soft as cats. You wouldn't have heard a boot scrape, not a breath. And there was Lovell pre-parin' himself for a quiet night; pot of coffee, some decent jerky, swig or two from his bottle once the fire came through. Time to be alone under the stars — '

'Then we swooped!' grinned Free-man, thudding a fist to a waiting palm. 'Swooped like eagles. And in an instant he was ours.'

'He never moved,' said Smith, taking up the narrative with a swagger across the boardwalk. 'Hardly had the time to breathe. You know somethin', folks, I reckon as how he had a premonition of bein' taken, like he knew his time was up.'

'And it was,' added Freeman, 'and how! Yessir. He hardly moved; raised his arms, and gave himself up. He knew well enough when to call it a day. He had been taken, as close to bein' with his pants down as made no odds!'

Smith swaggered again. 'One bad move and we would've shot him right there, make no mistake to that. Shot him like a dog.'

'Like the dog he still is,' echoed Freeman.

The crowd stayed silent, gazing, some open-mouthed, some sweating without feeling the heat. No one seemed to move. Even the flies had ceased to dart and buzz.

Sheriff McConnell scanned the faces, judging his moment to put an end to the proceedings. 'So there you have it, folks, straight from the horses' mouths, so to speak. These men were there and they did it, and for that we should all be grateful. They have succeeded in ridding this territory — '

'How come Lovell was alone out there?' called a voice from deep in the crowd.

McConnell glanced first at Freeman then at Smith. Neither man offered an answer.

'Yeah, how come?' echoed another voice. 'Mite strange, ain't it, for a fella who seemed to surround himself with guns? I heard tell as how the scumbag never moved without a half-dozen sidekicks standin' in his shadow.'

The crowd began to murmur. Men turned to the fellow next to him to voice an opinion, relate some tale he had heard told of Jude Lovell.

'Well, now, I guess we ain't goin' to have an answer to that question, are we?' smiled McConnell. 'Who's to say? Who can get to the thinkin' in a mind

21

such as Lovell's? But, who knows, mebbe he'll tell us before we hang him!' He raised his arms again. 'And now let's clear the street, eh, folks? Let's give these worthy fellas a chance to rest up awhiles. I guess they'll be more than happy to meet you all later on.'

The sheriff ushered Freeman and Smith back to his office, ordered his deputies to ensure that the street cleared peacefully and quickly and mopped a huge bandanna over his face.

The fellow in the crowd had made a valid point, he thought, adjusting his hat. Why had Lovell been alone? Where had he been heading, and why? There had to be a reason. Somebody must know.

Who was that somebody? Where was he?

4

Marshal Brand had ridden into Saracen, weaved his way down the crowded street where the early evening drinkers were assembling at the Garter Saloon, hitched his horse outside the sheriff's office, dusted himself down and mounted the board-walk to the half-open door, when the first shots rang out like spits of storm lightning.

He ducked on instinct, then fell back in the full force of the bodies pouring from the office.

He sprawled helpless for a moment on his butt, his fingers scrambling to push himself upright again, blinked and gaped at the bulk of the sheriff and the thin-lipped deputy glowering over him.

'You lookin' for me, fella?' growled McConnell. 'Well, it'll have to wait awhiles. I gotta town full of hot-heads and half-drunk drifters all steamed up for a hangin' and there ain't no place for shootin'. So, sorry, you're goin' to have to wait. Come back later.'

And with that the sheriff and his deputy had stepped over the still sprawled body of Marshal Brand and launched themselves into the bustling, dust-hazed street.

It was a full half-minute before Brand was upright and steady on his feet again, dusting himself down for a second time and wishing to hell he had taken his retirement a whole lot earlier.

He removed his hat, skimmed the dirt from the brim and was about to step down to the street when a third figure appeared in the doorway. He wiped the sweat and dust from his face and took a deeper breath. 'Evenin', ma'am,' he smiled, fumbling the hat through his hands. 'I wasn't expectin' . . .'

He stared at the woman facing him, his eyes narrowing. She was well dressed, he thought, even by Saracen standards. Expensively dressed, in fact.

The drape of her gown was lavish and tailored. There was a hint of jewellery, the drift of heady but not trashy perfume. His gaze moved to the woman's face: blue eyes, full lips, cared for skin, rich dark hair that collected the vague shimmers of light to it. 'Yeah . . . like I said, ma'am, I wasn't — '

'You wouldn't be Marshal Brand, would you?' Her eyes danced across him. The lips parted in a generous smile. 'You would! I can tell a marshal at a glance!' She extended a hand. 'Hedda Folde. My husband Charlton owns the Garter. Delighted to meet you, Marshal. I'd heard — we'd all heard — you were coming, of course, but had no idea when. We have a room set aside for you.' She broke from the marshal's lingering — probably nervous — handshake and eased the smile away to a not very convincing frown. 'But what a reception!' A hand went dramatically to her mouth as if to stifle embarrassment. 'What you must think — '

More shots spat across the gathering night. Brand swung round to the street, a hand dropping instinctively to his holstered Colt.

'Oh, pay no heed to that,' said the woman, swishing across the boardwalk to take Brand's elbow in a tight grip. 'Come with me. I'll have someone look to your horse. We have things to discuss.' She led the marshal to the street. 'Clear a way there,' she ordered in a high demanding voice. 'Clear a way.'

'Best look to your place in a hurry, ma'am,' called a man from the throng. 'Shootin's comin' from there. New faces in town.'

The woman halted abruptly, her hand dropping from Brand's elbow. 'Who?' she asked, her eyes flashing. 'Would I know them?'

'Very likely,' said a thin man in a jacket two sizes too large for him. 'They're from back East, lady, or so I hear. Your part of the world.'

Hedda Folde grunted, the full lips tightening as she pushed ahead again,

Brand in her swishing wake.

Another shot. A grunted moan.

'Stand clear, ma'am,' said Brand, drawing his Colt. 'Sounds to me like this is law business. I'll handle it.'

'Damned if you will, Marshal,' snapped the woman, reaching the boardwalk to the 'wings. 'I'm obliged, but these are my premises and I'll deal — '

Sheriff McConnell burst through the 'wings in a jumble of limbs, torn and bloodstained shirt. His fingers clutched like a crimson claw at the wound in his upper arm. His deputy staggered behind him.

'What the devil's going on in there, Mr McConnell?' demanded the woman.

The sheriff turned a wet, dirt-stained stare directly on her. 'What the hell's it look like, lady?' he croaked. 'I've got a half-crazed — '

The batwings creaked and swung again as a tall, wild-eyed, unshaven, long-haired man stepped to the boardwalk, twin Colts ranged menacingly in his grip.

Hedda Folde's mouth opened, but she made no sound. Sheriff McConnell winced as blood dripped freely from his arm to the boards. His deputy gulped and sweated until his face gleamed like hot grease. The crowd fell silent. They seemed suddenly incapable of movement. They simply watched and waited.

'Mooney,' said Brand, in a tone that bit on the air as if jaws had snapped.

The man stiffened, his face draining of the snarl. A slow, leering grin began to break across his cracked lips. He looked at Brand from the corner of his eyes and seemed to wait minutes before speaking, his gaze finally levelling on the marshal.

'Might've known,' he said slowly, the Colts loose in his grip at his sides. 'Should've guessed it.' He tittered. 'Marshal Brand. Again! Damnit, you're always there. Every time. Everywhere. You! Again and again and again . . . How'd you do it, Marshal? How'd you manage to keep croppin' up in my life like a hangover's bad taste? Tell me.'

Brand shrugged calmly, his stare steady. 'Persistence,' he smiled. 'I'm a persistent man.'

'You can say that again, Marshal,' leered the man, 'and you know somethin', I'm gettin' tired of your sonofabitch persistence. Real tired. So tired in fact I've a mind to —'

The twin Colts were suddenly raised, levelled, ranged, ready to spit their fire. But already too late as the marshal's gun blazed. Once. Twice. Then no more. Then only the return to silence.

Brand stepped closer to gaze directly into the man's face, as ugly in death as it had been in life. 'Frank Mooney,' he murmured. 'Now just what brought you here, I wonder?'

★ ★ ★

Sheriff McConnell slumped in the chair behind his desk, placed his hands on the cluttered top where a half-empty bottle of whiskey and glasses fought for their own space, thought about taking another measure, but instead sighed and lifted his tired gaze to the face of Marshal Brand.

'Sorry about before,' he said, in an equally tired voice, 'didn't recognize you in all that shootin' mayhem. First we've had. Folk have generally been level-headed in spite of all the rowdyin' and roosterin' on account of the hangin' comin' up. Never thought we'd come to that, an out-and-out shootin'. Hell, we're in serious territory here. If things get out of hand . . . ' He eyed the whiskey hungrily. 'But, even so, I ain't so sure, Marshal, about what you're tellin' me. I mean, one single member of Lovell's former gang — *just one*, and a dead one now at that — here in Saracen don't signify . . . '

He winced at the sudden stab of pain through his wounded arm, cursed, then reached for the bottle and poured a measure to the glass. 'Help yourself,' he nodded to Brand.

'You go easy on that liquor, Sheriff,' said Doc Munday, raising himself from a chair in the corner of the office. 'Nasty wound you've got there. Don't wanna go sousin' yourself in whiskey. Don't work, anyhow.' He snapped his medicine bag shut and moved to the open door. 'Not that you'll take a blind bit of notice.' He glanced at the marshal. 'Lawmen don't. It's a fact. Law unto themselves, you might say.' He sniffed and shrugged. 'Best go look to the rest of this heavin' town. Sooner we're shut of that prisoner you've got back there, the better.'

Doc Munday left and McConnell poured another whiskey.

'I ain't for speculatin' or spreadin' doubt,' said Brand, crossing to the office window to watch the street beyond it, 'but the fact that Mooney was here at all after all these years . . .' He turned sharply. 'Frank Mooney hadn't ridden with Lovell for close on three years. He pulled clear after the Ashcroft raid. So why was he here tonight? Why ride all those miles — for what? To watch his old partner dancin' at the end of a rope? Just that?'

'What else?' asked one of the newly recruited team of special guards hired for the sole purpose of a round-the-clock watch over Jude Lovell. He closed the door to the cells quietly behind him and nodded to McConnell. 'All quiet back there. Lovell's still broodin'. Art's taken my place.'

The sheriff grunted and watched as Brand turned back to the window.

'I don't know what else,' said the marshal. 'I have no idea. But I just don't like the sight of Frank Mooney in a town, 'specially this town, dead or alive. It don't bode well in my experience.'

Sheriff McConnell winced again, touched his bound wound softly as if to shield it, and came slowly to his feet. 'Well, mebbe you're right, Marshal. I ain't for passin' judgement. All I do know is that I've got one helluva heavin' town out there, sort of town where anythin' might happen, as I'm sure you appreciate. And I've got Jude

Lovell at my back. Frankly, I'm plain dog-tired and fed up to my back braces with the whole outfit.

'But, this is my job, my responsibility and Saracen's my town, so I'm payin' due regard to what you're sayin' and to that marshal's badge you're wearin' there. Badges like that don't come easy.' He paused a moment to finger his wound again and eye the waiting whiskey bottle. 'I'll have my men keep a closer watch on who's in town and any new arrivals. Anythin' suspicious, you'll hear about it. Meantime, you've a room at the Garter. You've already met Mrs Folde. She was here to warn them bounty hunters to go easy on the town 'facilities', as she put it.' His gaze on the marshal deepened. 'Hedda Folde is the unofficial eyes and ears of Saracen. What she don't know about who's here ain't worth knowin'. Pay her heed, Marshal. She might be worth it.'

He paused a moment, let the deeper gaze lighten and added, 'You wanna take a look at Lovell?'

'He'll keep,' said Brand. 'I'll be here early tomorrow.' He adjusted his hat, crossed to the door and opened it. 'Keep watchin',' he murmured, and stepped away to the boardwalk.

McConnell sighed. 'Marshals — ain't they just another breed! Hell, as if I ain't got enough to cope with.' He turned to the off-duty guard. 'Care to join me in a drink? It's goin' to be a long night.'

5

The shooting of Frank Mooney had changed the mood of Saracen and its bustling throng of folk. Voices were suddenly quieter, conversations sober and a deal more thoughtful. For most the name Mooney meant nothing. No one had taken to the fellow with his arrogant swagger and demanding manner. Most, if they were honest, had been a touch scared of the man. He had looked like trouble, sounded like trouble, even smelled like trouble.

But now he was dead, gunned down in a straight shoot-out by Marshal Lyle Brand. More importantly for many he had been out-shot, out-thought by a whole sight faster gun. A very fast gun. A gun that might well prove deadly. Certainly a gun you would not be for arguing with.

And those of that opinion were of a

generally friendly and welcoming nature.

'It's good to know there's a marshal in town. Better still, when you know he can shoot. And fast!'

''Specially with the hangin' comin' up. Who's to say how much vermin Lovell might attract. Hell, he spent all his life among it.'

'But how many more like Mooney are there?'

'Yeah, how many? How we goin' to know 'em?'

'Could have half his old gang here come the hangin' day.'

'Mebbe that marshal'll know 'em . . . '

But Brand was saying nothing as he made his way along the busy street that night. He declined a score of offers to 'share a table and bottle' and shook his head politely at the barrage of questions that tumbled and jumbled around him:

'Did you figure for that rat Mooney bein' here, Marshal?'

'When did you first cross him?'

'You were fast back there, Marshal. How many men you killed?'

'You been trailin' Lovell these past years, Marshal?'

'Bet you wished you'd crossed him in the Bigbones, eh?'

'Would you have shot him on sight?'

'Mebbe hangin's too good for the scumbag . . . '

Brand had smiled, nodded, shrugged, but stayed silent. Hands slapped his back, patted his shoulders. A man with a bulging paunch and a handful of cigars had stuffed three in his vest pocket. A young girl had blown him a kiss and struggled to get closer. Two men had offered to buy his gun for any price he cared to name. Another said he would pay in gold for his hat.

The normally five-minute walk from the sheriff's office to the Garter had taken nearly thirty by the time Brand mounted the boardwalk to the 'wings — noting as he did so the areas of scrubbed bloodstains — to be greeted by mine hosts, Hedda and Charlton Folde.

It was the woman who stepped

forward to greet him in a wafting shroud of perfume, her smile wide and unbroken, her eyes flashing.

'This way,' she clipped, leading him towards a door marked Private at the far end of the bar while her husband nodded and headed for the bar.

Brand went willingly and easily enough, anxious now to be out of the pushing crowds, the sea of staring eyes, the throb of voices. His gaze moved quickly over the dozens of faces thronging the bar: well-dressed men of almost any professional calling; the not so fortunate; the drifters, scroungers, those looking to make a quick dollar; those working the tables for a free drink, the half-smoked cigar, the loose change left carelessly within easy reach.

Women and girls; some with partners, some very obviously alone, but with a hopeful, sometimes desperate, eye for the lucky chance. The Garter's bar girls were not without a steady stream of customers, all carefully monitored by Charlton Folde, as he did the bar where trade never seemed to slacken and the liquor flowed as if from a creek stream.

The air was thick and yellow with smoke, the smells a heady mixture of booze, cigars, sweat and cheap scent.

Brand noted the hired heavyweights, the troubleshooters, moving watchfully among the tables. Three stayed close to what he took to be the two bounty hunters who had brought Lovell in. They drew an attentive audience, but one not without questions and their own pointed observations, some of which the hunters answered — how truthfully, wondered Brand? — some they fended off, some they dismissed entirely. The hunters nodded as the marshal passed, their eyes, he thought, following him. Or did he imagine that?

They reached the door to the private room and went in.

Lavish, mused Brand, his gaze taking in the furnishings, decoration, paintings, ornaments; much like Hedda Folde. Nothing but the best. He would not have expected other. The room was dimly lit from a single lantern's glow to the left of the main table where glasses awaited decanters of whiskey, wine and brandy.

Brand grunted quietly to himself, as if to clear his throat, and waited for the woman to take up her position with her back to the room's single window, the lantern light at its most strategic to display her at her most dazzling.

'You've had a busy arrival,' said the woman, her smile soft, the gaze steady but not deep. 'You knew the man Mooney. Lucky for us you did, Mr Brand. No saying to the trouble he might have caused. We are grateful to you.'

Brand said nothing. There was nothing to say. She, along with half the town, had seen the shooting. It had been fair, well within the law. As far as he was concerned it had simply been the end of Frank Mooney. Good riddance.

'We are well clear of such men,' said

Hedda Folde, echoing Brand's thoughts. She poured two generous measures of a quality brandy and handed one to the Marshal. 'He had ridden with Lovell, I hear,' she went on.

'Sometime back, ma'am,' offered Brand. 'Years ago. Not recently.'

'Odd he should turn up here. Almost morbid if all he came to see was his one-time partner hang. Don't you think so, Marshal?'

'Mebbe,' shrugged Brand. 'Such men ain't for bein' reckoned in normal terms.'

The woman smiled. 'As you say. I'm sure you've seen such behaviour many times before.' The smile faded. 'Might there be others with a similar curiosity?'

'Others?' frowned Brand. 'You mean from Lovell's gang? Here to see him hang?'

The woman raised her eyebrows and deepened her gaze.

'It's possible,' said Brand carefully, wondering where the question was leading and why it had been asked.

41

'Many men rode with Lovell. Some still are his close partners. He fell out with a handful of the closest, but for every one lost there were three waiting to fill their boots. Lovell is that kind of fella. He commands a devoted loyalty.'

Hedda Folde sampled her drink delicately, then replaced it on the table in front of her. She seemed to lapse into thought for a moment. 'Some men do,' she murmured, as if to herself. Her eyes flashed. 'What do you know of Ben Pullman, Matt Michaels, Colorado Jack, Joe Doone, and the one they call the Dealer?'

'Hold on there, ma'am,' said Brand, urging the woman to halt. 'Them's names that ain't for mentionin' lightly, much less tanglin' with. Every one of 'em is or has been one of Lovell's men. They've all ridden with him. Colorado Jack still does, and I hear told of how the Dealer's back in the gang.' He felt a beading of sweat across his brow. 'Hell, ma'am, they're all wanted men in their own right, to the last. But like I say, not one is for tanglin' with. Killers, the whole pack of 'em, and they ain't fussy who they're killin'. Women just as easy as men. In fact . . . '

He paused, his voice drifting into silence. He finished his drink in a single gulp and narrowed his gaze on Hedda Folde's almost expressionless face where, for the first time that night, there was the faintest trace of grey.

'Why are you askin', ma'am?' asked Brand, his voice suddenly dry as blown dirt.

'Because they're all here, Marshal,' said the woman. 'In Saracen. Sharing rooms in this saloon!'

6

Brand heard the grind and thud of a clock marking the half-hour. The noises of the bar beyond the room — voices, clink of glasses, laughter, girls' giggles — blurred to a distant hum. The light from the lantern seemed to dim to a softer, almost nervous glow.

He swallowed. 'Here?' he mumbled, floundering to confirm what he had just heard. 'In Saracen . . . ' He swallowed again, his throat aching on the dryness. 'You're sure? How can you be so sure?'

Hedda Folde turned to a box on a sideboard to her right, opened it, selected a long, tightly rolled cheroot, lit it and blew a pencil-thin line of smoke through her full, damp lips. 'Because, Mr Brand, I've seen all of them in my time. Years ago, of course, before all this, the luxuries of Charlton

Folde's money, the Garter, my expertise in running it.' She blew another line of smoke, waited for it to curl and break across the ceiling, then smiled and said, 'Don't be under any illusions, Marshal, what you see now hasn't always been so.

'Time was when I too was a sassy bar girl, just like any one of those out there right now. But I had ambition. I was going places. I never worked a saloon longer than a year, then I'd move on; some new town, a fresh territory, maybe a whole new state. Consequently, I got to see and know an awful lot of folk.

'The likes of Pullman, Michaels, Colorado Jack, Joe Doone . . . I crossed their path, had some of them in my bed. But, like I say, that was some time back. Point is — '

'The point is,' said Brand, snapping into life, 'if they're here, as you say they are, have they recognized you? Have you spoken to them?'

The woman thought for a moment. Smoke curled. Her gaze softened. The room seemed bathed in its own silence. 'Perhaps they've recognized me, yes, but we certainly haven't spoken. Not yet.'

'Hell,' mouthed the marshal, his mind beginning to spin, his thoughts to teem. 'More to the point perhaps, why are they all here now? To see Lovell hang? Just that? To witness somethin' like a bizarre sideshow? Or is there another reason?'

There was a soft tap at the door, a pause, and then the click as it opened and Charlton Folde sidled into the room as if trying to dodge his own shadow.

'Don't want half the town knowin' we're all here,' he said, a faint grin sliding over his lips like ice. 'They'll get nosy. They always get nosy.' He moved deeper into the room. 'Has she told you?' he asked quietly, fingering the silk cravat at his neck before smoothing the cut of his velvet-faced jacket. 'About Lovell's men? About them bein' here?' A frown deepened across his brow. His gaze darkened. 'What do you reckon, Marshal? There's more to it than meets the eye, isn't there?'

* * *

Perhaps there was. Perhaps there was a whole sight more to it than either the Foldes, the marshal, or anybody else who had noticed their presence in town, had reckoned. But figuring it might not be so easy. Not, thought Brand twenty minutes later, as he made his way from the private room to a comparatively quiet end of the Garter's sprawling bar, if you wanted to stay alive.

At the first hint of threat, the likes of Colorado Jack, Joe Doone and any one of the others of the original Lovell gang, fired fast, first and without question. It was their code. No risks, no loose chances. The survival of one secured the lives of all.

But what precisely? Clearly the Foldes, and doubtless many others of Saracen's leading citizenry, would expect Brand to do something. He was, after all, a territorial marshal. He had authority, respect, power. Did they figure on Brand arresting the bunch, one by one, until they were all behind bars awaiting trial and the inevitable rope? A move like that would prelude a bloodbath before the cell door had clanged shut on the first one arrested.

Sheriff McConnell would have to be brought fully into the picture, of course. But how far would the sheriff want to go given the limited range of his deputies? Should Brand send north for more guns; deputies with experience and equally fast guns? That would take time.

How soon before Lovell's one-time partners recognized Brand? Would they leave him alone? Plot to kill him? Would it be a fast shot from the shadows, or the silent swish of a blade in the night?

Supposing, he pondered, easing his hands round the glass of a cool beer, the bunch were here to spring their leader at the last minute; maybe wait until Judge Whinnie had pronounced judgment, and then spring their one-time leader, almost as the hangman was slipping the noose round Lovell's neck.

But whatever their purpose, however many of them gathered with whatever plan to ensure Jude Lovell's escape, the same question returned again and again to nag at the marshal's thoughts: why had Jude Lovell been alone in the Bigbones?

He had posed the question to the Foldes, but neither had offered an explanation. Charlton Folde had shrugged and fingered his jacket. His wife had opened her mouth to say something, then thought better of it — which had been the moment for Brand to ease away.

He had thanked them for the information, trusted they would continue to keep a careful watch on the situation and assured them he would see them again in the morning. Meantime . . .

He had felt Hedda Folde's eyes on his back, even when he had closed the door on the room and returned to the smoke-hazed bar, and had the uncomfortable feeling they would be there while ever he was in Saracen.

He dismissed the thought again as he finished the beer and made his way briskly from the bar to the street.

He needed to talk to Sheriff McConnell. Right now, whatever the hour.

* * *

The street was less crowded but still busy. Heads turned as the marshal pushed open the 'wings and left the saloon. Some men waved, a group shouted their encouragement; a bar girl taking the air on the boardwalk wished him a friendly goodnight; a drunk with his legs dangling from the walk to the dusty street, raised bloodshot eyes, slurred a greeting then went back to sleep.

Brand hurried on, more conscious

now of the shadows and what they might hold, his eyes scanning faces with a new urgency. The next one to turn his way might be that of Ben Pullman, Matt Michaels, Colorado Jack . . . He quickened his pace, reached the sheriff's office and pushed open the door.

'Before you say it, I've heard,' said McConnell, crossing the office to the cabinet where he housed his liquor supply. 'An hour back. Had half the town committee here.' He turned from the cabinet, an unopened bottle of whiskey in his grip. 'Lovell's men are in town.' He crossed to his desk, sat down, opened the bottle and poured two measures to waiting glasses. 'Guessed you'd hear the news from Hedda Folde, so I was expectin' you.' He offered a glass to Brand. 'What's your thinkin'?'

'We stay quiet for the time bein'. Wait and see. Anythin' else might put a spark to a powder keg.'

McConnell grunted and sampled his drink. 'Figured you'd reckon that. Makes sense — but, hell, the powder keg itself is a mite dauntin'. We're goin' to be livin' on a blade edge.' He finished the drink, slid the glass to the table, sat back and steepled his fingers. 'Trouble is, there might be more on the way. You figure on them plannin' to spring Lovell?'

'It's likely,' said Brand. 'And yet . . . ' He stared into the drink. 'I can't be sure.' He waited a moment. 'Tighten the guard. Keep Lovell under watch round-the-clock. No slackin'. Once Judge Whinnie gets here — '

A man sporting a battered derby that threatened to spill from his head like a bucket, stumbled into the office, gasped, swallowed, settled his hat, and blurted, 'It's your deputy, Sheriff, the one with the scar down his cheek.'

'John Bowen,' said McConnell.

'Him.' The man swallowed again, took a deep breath, and went on, 'He's dead. Just found him. Back of the mercantile. Been stabbed, clean through the neck.'

7

Sheriff McConnell's deputy was indeed dead and had been for some time in the opinion of Doc Munday who took only minutes to conclude his examination. 'Attacked from behind,' he pronounced, stepping carefully round the body. 'Two, mebbe three hours back. Wouldn't have felt a thing.' He raised his eyes to the sheriff's face. 'Nasty,' he added. 'But the work of a professional even so. Whoever killed this poor devil had done it before, probably many times.' He collected his medicine bag. 'We've got a knife man in town. Know any?'

Pullman, thought Brand, watching from the edge of the crowd that had gathered at the rear of the store. Ben Pullman had always been a speciality blade man. Could trim a fly's wings with a knife at fifteen feet, was one of the more fanciful claims made for him.

The men in the crowd began to murmur among themselves, some speculating on the strange characters who had swelled the already teeming population of the town; some favouring a drunk for the killing, or maybe somebody in dispute with the deputy over a woman, or any one of a heap of reasons men have for falling foul of another.

'Hell,' chipped one young wag, 'what they tryin' to do here — prelude the main event with some side killin's!'

A man threw a punch that felled the wag in an instant. Nobody went to his aid.

Brand waited until the sheriff had completed his own examination of the body and made the necessary arrangements for its removal before moving quietly to his side.

'One of Lovell's gang, has to be,' he murmured, beyond earshot of the town men. 'Takin' their revenge after losin' Mooney. They figure things that way. This'll be the work of Ben Pullman. He was always the gang's knife man.'

McConnell grunted but made no reply as store-keeper Jim Squire and banker Milton Boyd pushed their way through the crowd to join him.

'Bad business,' said Squire, acknowledging Brand with a quick nod.

'Very,' echoed Boyd, clouding his face in a swirl of cigar smoke. 'Town's gettin' dangerous, too dangerous for comfort. I suggest the committee meets early tomorrow, before we open for business.' He consulted a lavishly engraved timepiece. 'Shall we say the bank, seven-thirty? You'll be welcome to join us, Marshal. We'll be needin' your experience, I fancy.'

The men watched in silence as the body of the deputy was carried away. It was Squire who was the first to speak.

'We need to get this whole Lovell business over and done with,' he said, a note of urgency clipping his words. 'If that darned circuit Judge don't arrive soon, this town'll erupt. You hear me, Sheriff? It'll blow up in our faces.'

★ ★ ★

It was the persistent tapping at the door of his room that stirred Brand from a deep, dreamless sleep.

He waited a moment, his body stretched full length on the bed; listening, blinking as his eyes opened fully. It was still dark, somewhere in those lost hours between the depth of night and the slow gathering of a new day. He blinked again; shadows began to reveal shapes, none of them familiar; he defined the area of a window, the faint chinks of light where the drapes had not met, a dressing-table, chair. Memory caught up with him. He was in bluegrass country, in the town of Saracen. Jude Lovell . . . Sheriff McConnell . . . crowds of people, Frank Mooney . . . the stabbing of a deputy . . . Lovell's men.

The tapping was repeated, insistent, urgent. He grunted an acknowledgement, heaved himself from the bed and crossed unsteadily to the door.

'Marshal? You there? Marshal Brand?'

He recognized the voice of Hedda Folde, frowned, grunted and fumbled for his pants. 'Hang on there,' he called, desperate to recall where the room's lantern had been placed. 'Give me a minute.'

He dressed, found the lantern, lit it and crossed back to the door. There had better be a very good reason for waking me at this hour, he thought, turning the knob.

Hedda Folde looked almost as glittering as she had earlier that night; the same immaculate fold to her dress, not a strand of hair out of place; her eyes bright and as probing as ever. But her attempt at a soft smile failed miserably. 'Sorry to wake you, Marshal,' she began, glancing anxiously to the left, then to the right of the dimly lit corridor. 'I figured you should know.'

Brand frowned. 'Know what?' he croaked, in a voice still struggling from sleep.

'Lovell's men,' she hissed, as if

expecting the walls to press closer to catch her words. 'Pullman, Michaels, Joe Doone, Colorado Jack, the Dealer . . . they've pulled out. Saddled up and headed West. I watched them leave their rooms.'

She swallowed. Her eyes flashed, darted to the shadows, came back to the marshal's face in a deeper, darker stare. 'Why? What the hell they figuring?'

'McConnell know?' asked Brand.

'One of his men on patrol saw them. Jess Morden from the livery is downstairs with McConnell right now.'

'Give me a couple of minutes and I'll be with you,' said Brand.

★   ★   ★

'What's it mean — they gotten cold feet or somethin'? Mebbe we scared them off, eh?'

Sheriff McConnell's words fell across a tired silence in the gloomy bar of the Garter saloon as he paced from one wall to the other, pausing only to glance quickly over the faces watching him.

Hedda Folde, resplendent in a lavish crimson gown, which seemed to flare as if in mockery of the new day still hours away, stood impassively remote, her eyes fixed on the almost empty street. Her husband counted the night's takings at a corner table, his lips moving silently to the steady skim of his fingers through notes. A handful of drunks, lost in the worlds of their sodden slumber, sprawled at a long table at the back of the bar. Nobody had the interest or the strength to move them. They would wake when business resumed.

Jess Morden, a heavily built bulk of a man who owned and ran the town livery, stood with his arms folded to the side of the batwings. A newly sworn sheriff's deputy ran his hands nervously over the stock of a Winchester. Jim Squire twirled a timepiece round a finger, halted it, then reversed the swing.

McConnell lit a cheroot and blew the smoke thoughtfully. 'What do you reckon, Marshal?'

Brand eased himself from the shadows into the glow of the only lit lantern. He gazed over the waiting faces, heard the near imperceptible hum of life in an over-crowded town that could not, or would not sleep, and wondered what the hell he was doing here. He should be sleeping, dreaming of a river, its swirls and eddies, the fish beneath them . . .

'They ain't ridin' this early for their health,' he heard himself saying. 'And they ain't runnin' neither. Why should they? Ain't neither me nor the Sheriff here approached any one of 'em over the knifin' of that deputy. In fact, we ain't done or said a thing to 'em. So they up and out on a whim at this hour. Why? Where to?' He turned to the livery owner. 'I hear they headed west: that a fact?'

'West, no doubtin' to it,' confirmed Morden.

'They say anything'?' asked the marshal.

Jess shrugged, his arms still folded. 'The one they call the Dealer thanked me for lookin' to their horses, asked to the cost and paid me. Straight up. No fussin'.'

'Paid you!' snapped McConnell, his head lost in a sudden surge of cheroot smoke. 'Types like them, they paid you?'

'That's right. And added five dollars for my kindly trouble.'

McConnell coughed smoke, blinked his tired, sore, bloodshot eyes and wheezed. 'Darn it, if I ain't heard everythin'! What in the name of bluegrass sanity is happenin' round here? Somebody tell me, f'Chris'sake!'

'Check on the security guardin' Lovell,' said Brand sharply, making his way to the 'wings, 'then come with me.'

'Where we goin'?' spluttered the sheriff, wafting aside the thickening smoke.

'We're ridin' — West!'

8

They rode fast and hard through a night not yet done and a day still in waiting. The trail west of Lovell's men had been easy to pick up and follow in its directness.

'One thing's for certain,' said McConnell, tightening his gaze as the cooler air in the momentum of the pace stung his eyes, 'they ain't fussed none about bein' followed.' He cracked the reins. 'What the hell they plannin'?'

'That's what we're here to find out,' answered Brand, narrowing his gaze on the shadows and shapes ahead.

'But supposin' they are just pullin' out?' persisted the sheriff. 'I ain't swallowin' no notion that they rode all the way here on the off-chance of puttin' a blade across the throat of one of my deputies. That don't wash in my book, not with types like them it don't. No, they were in Saracen for a purpose, botherin' nobody, just visitin' along of half the territory all set for Lovell's hangin', but there with somethin' special in mind. No doubtin' that. And I ain't persuaded other.' He cracked the reins again. 'Mebbe, they were figurin' on springin' Lovell. Mebbe the crowded town put them off. Mebbe the shootin' of Mooney changed their minds.' He grinned to himself. 'Hey, mebbe it was you, Marshal. Could be they hadn't reckoned on crossin' you.'

Brand offered no comment as the ride deepened, the pale glow of Saracen faded at their backs and the rougher country to the foothills of the Bigbones spread round them like something disputing their presence.

'It's the mountains,' clipped McConnell, peering ahead intently. 'That's their destination.'

'Crossin' them, or just reachin' them?' asked Brand.

McConnell shot him a quick glance. 'What's that supposed to mean?'

'Just that.'

'Well, I ain't got an answer, mister, not to hand, anyhow.' The sheriff huffed quietly. 'Best get to concentratin'. Light ain't nothin' like up yet and the goin's gettin' rougher. But I figure we're still close enough to keep track.'

They were swallowed almost instantly by the half-night, half-day gloom.

★ ★ ★

It was close on another five miles of hard riding before Brand indicated a drift of rock and boulders and reined towards it.

'Time to ease up,' he said, wiping a bandanna over his face. Sheriff McConnell slid from his saddle and relaxed his mount. 'See anythin'?' asked Brand. 'Hear anythin'?'

McConnell concentrated for a moment. 'Nothin',' he pronounced at last. 'I'd figure they've reined up some place.' He listened again. 'If they were still ridin' we'd pick up the hoofbeat at this hour and specially out here.'

'What's up ahead; anywhere they might have agreed to stage a meetin'?'

McConnell thought for a moment. 'Coupla places come to mind,' he mused. 'Chance Creek. Bearpaw Cut. Either of 'em deep hidden.' He frowned. 'You reckonin' on the characters meetin' more of the same scum?'

'It's possible. Guess anythin's possible, but I just get the feelin' — '

'Bearpaw Cut,' said McConnell remounting. 'If I was out here lookin' on a meetin', that'd be my choice. 'Bout a mile dead ahead. Single line track, so go steady.'

Brand grunted and followed the sheriff clear of the drift and back to the rough stone and scrub they had been crossing since leaving town. He shifted his gaze to the banks of dark cloud where night now was fast retreating and the brighter, stronger light of the new day beginning to show. Full light in another hour, he reckoned. And by then . . .

He had no idea what, if anything, they might find at Bearpaw Cut. If Lovell's men were there, had ridden out to a meeting, then just who were they meeting and why? A sudden chill scudded down his spine. There was something wrong, something very wrong, in all this, but he could not for the life of him, and for all his years of experience, put his finger on it.

If the likes of Pullman, Colorado Jack, Michaels, Doone and the Dealer were planning a dramatic last minute escape for Lovell, then hell, how many guns did they need to pull it off? Pullman, Colorado and Joe Doone alone could handle a heist like that. So where did that leave . . . ?

He swallowed, clicked the reins through his fingers and hissed a curse through his teeth. Of course, damn it, he had missed the obvious. What was the Dealer doing here? The Dealer only ever figured in anything Lovell and his gang were planning when —

'Bearpaw Cut. Two minutes away,' called McConnell softly. 'Suggest we approach on foot. You reckon?'

*　*　*

They went like scurrying dawn insects over the stone, rocks and clinging scrub, the light breaking steadily across the long eastern skies. It would be only minutes now before they made shadows; and when shadows moved and were seen by watchful eyes, trigger fingers got itchy.

McConnell eased an arm from his side to urge Brand to halt. The two men crouched only yards apart. They watched, waited and listened. No sounds, no movements. How deep into the hills had Lovell's men gone, wondered Brand; had they left a lookout? He scanned what he could make out of the steady slope to the foothills ahead. A man could stay hidden and unseen here for hours. But would the riders who had left town so hurriedly and unexpectedly have reckoned on being followed?

McConnell hissed for Brand's attention and pointed to the blurred outline of a ridge some distance away. 'There,' he mouthed, and moved on.

Brand scrambled in his wake, annoyed with himself when he sent a rock tumbling into the looser stone and froze for a moment at the eerie clatter of it. He swallowed. No response. If a lookout had been posted, he was keeping low and silent.

McConnell waited, turned to give Brand the thumbsup, then shifted again, this time going lower, almost on all-fours as he scrambled for hand and footholds without disturbing the screes and pebbles.

The vague new light spread like something poured across the peaks and rocks. The air lost its dawn chill. Brand felt the first trickle of sweat across his back, beading on his brow. The place would be a hell-hole come full sun-up, he thought, dismissing the image immediately. Why did that river, his retirement cabin and the hazy days of fishing for lazy fish suddenly seem so far away? Why had it been his bad luck for Jude Lovell to be captured now, in the Bigbones, within such easy reach of Saracen?

It was then that he hissed another curse through his teeth and could have kicked himself if a leg had been available to inflict it. 'Damn!' he muttered, pausing to adjust his hat and wondering if he should call McConnell back to hear his figuring. Maybe not — at least not yet, not out here with the light growing in strength and the shadows beginning to build. McConnell was intent on the distant ridge. He pushed on.

Twenty minutes later they were resting, catching their breath, wiping the sweat from their faces within a few feet of the top of the ridge. Brand stayed silent on his thoughts.

'I figure that if Lovell's scum are

here, we'll be able to catch a sight of 'em from the ridge,' said McConnell. 'If they're goin' deeper or higher, well, I guess we'll have to let 'em go. Can't be away from town for too long. There's too much at stake back there — includin' my reputation! Yours along of me, come to that. Hell, we don't want to go down in history as the men who couldn't keep Jude Lovell penned! In any case, circuit Judge Whinnie should be gettin' close.' He drew his Colt. 'Shall we go take a look?'

★   ★   ★

They squirmed on their stomachs to the rim of the ridge. At first there was little of shape and substance to be seen. A low morning mist hugged the depths of the creek below them. Rock and stone shelved steeply for a few yards before easing to gentle slopes which, from here at this hour, were lost in the creep of mist.

But not entirely.

Brand blinked, cleared his eyes, narrowed them and placed a hand on McConnell's arm. 'Down there,' he murmured. 'To your right, far as you can see.' He waited. 'See 'em? Horses, riders.'

'Ben Pullman . . . Colorado Jack . . . I see 'em. And the others.' McConnell peered harder. 'Hell,' he hissed, 'there must be a dozen . . . fifteen . . . damnit, more like twenty. What in tarnation's goin' on?' His gaze tightened on Brand's face. A soft line of sweat glistened on his forehead in the shadow of the brim of his hat. He frowned. 'Do you know?' he asked, the hiss thickening to an almost gasping croak.

Brand indicated for the sheriff to ease back from the rim and return to where they had hitched their mounts.

Not until they were clear of the ridge and well beyond earshot of the creek did McConnell speak again. 'And now perhaps you'll tell me what is really goin' on in this crazy world I seem to have stepped into.' He wiped his dusty, sweat-streaked face with a bandanna that had seen better days.

'It's all a carefully staged plot,' Brand began. 'Lovell was in these mountains alone because that was the start of it; the bounty hunters who took him and brought him in, are known to him, members of his own gang.'

'But how — ?' blurted McConnell, letting the bandanna hang limp in his hand.

'Him bein' held in your jail, supposedly awaitin' trial, is a diversion, a hoax, dupe, call it what you will,' Brand continued, dismissing the sheriff's interruption. 'The real action is comin' from his gang of scumbag gunslingers back there in the creek. They're goin' to be your real trouble, Sheriff. They're the ones who are goin' to hit Saracen like a tornado and rip it to pieces. Losin' Lovell ain't goin' to be nothin' in the light of what's brewin' in Pullman's mind. And it's all been timed in detail, down to the last second.'

'What you tellin' me here?' croaked McConnell.

'Mount up and I'll explain on the way back,' said Brand. 'Time's already got a gun at our heads.'

9

The light shafted brightly through the window of the president's office at the County and Territories Bank. Particles of grey dust swirled through it as if caught in a silent vacuum. The air thickened; the day's heat deepened — and trouble, as far as Milton Boyd was concerned, grew almost as fast as the piles of cash and gold gathering in the bank's safes. The money he could handle; the trouble he was not so sure about.

He slumped back in the chair behind his bulbous oak desk, linked his fingers under his chin and stared at the men facing him: Jim Squire, Jess Morden, Doc Munday, Sheriff McConnell, Marshal Lyle Brand and Hedda Folde. They in their turn stared back, waiting, fearful and, in McConnell's case, with an anxious beading of sweat glistening on his face.

'I'm sorry, but I'm not one-hundred per cent convinced,' said Boyd at last, breaking the tension of the silence as if it had been dropped. 'I mean, where's the evidence? How can you be so certain? It isn't as if somebody's told you, or confessed. Have you asked Lovell outright? Put it to him point-blank: 'Are you and your men planning to raid the bank? How do you intend doin' it? When? And why have you allowed yourself to be taken prisoner?' It none of it makes any sense to me. At least, not right now it don't.'

'It sure as hell does to me,' snapped Squire, his lips set in a defiant straight line.

'Me too,' joined Jess Morden, folding his arms dramatically.

Doc Munday cleared his throat politely. 'I have to say that I was never completely happy with the manner in which Lovell was taken. Those two so-called bounty hunters never quite looked the part, and it all sounded a whole lot too easy. No, it raised questions and doubts. But as for Marshal Brand's theorizin' over the gatherin' of the men out there in the Bigbones, well, that all makes good sense. Lovell himself must have worked out what would happen here in Saracen once he was taken and the news spread. I would wager you're holdin' more money in your bank, Milton, than you have ever handled. Would I be right?'

The president sat forward, squirmed and flattened his hands on the desk. 'Well, that depends on — '

'I'll take that as a 'yes',' said Doc.

Hedda Folde swished the folds of her dress as she circled the desk and walked to the window overlooking the shaded boardwalk and already crowded main street. 'A perfect decoy,' she smiled to herself, swishing the dress again as if to emphasize the point. 'A handful of gunslingers spring Lovell while the rest are raiding the bank, stripping it clean down to the very bones and generally reducing the town to a state of mayhem with blood and lead flying everywhere.'

She swung round, circled the desk and rejoined the others, her stare as fixed as a beam on the bank president's face. 'If you can't see at least the possibilities of that happening right here in Saracen — and maybe fairly soon at that — you ain't worthy of taking responsibility for our hard-earned money.'

'Now wait a minute,' began Boyd, the blood colouring his cheeks as he came to his feet.

'Like the marshal here says,' the woman continued, 'there ain't the time for more waiting. Fact or imagination, we need to get moving. And don't say: go ask Lovell. I can imagine his reply!'

'Very well,' said Boyd, 'if what Hedda says is the feeling of you all — though I personally remain doubtful — then I must, in the interest of my customers and for the reputation and good standing at the bank, co-operate all I can.' He gazed at McConnell and Brand. 'What are you proposing we do, gentlemen?'

A fly swirled for a moment through the shafted beam of bright light.

★　★　★

Saracen was going about its by now familiar chaotic way by the time the meeting in Milton Boyd's office broke up and the folk involved went their separate ways to the thronging street, all well aware of what they had to do.

'I need men, and fast,' said McConnell, smothering his face in a vast bandanna as he hugged what he could of the crowded boardwalk shade.

Hedda Folde hurried back to the Garter saloon where she found her husband still counting through the piles of money flowing freely by the hour to the business coffers. She would draw neither help nor understanding by telling him of the marshal's discovery: Charlton's only concerns were the takings.

'Got to be straight up about it, my dear, the takin' of Jude Lovell has been one helluva boost for business. You should see these figures. Do you have any idea of the money we've taken on the girls alone? At this rate, I'll — I mean we'll — be retirin' inside another year. I'm tellin' you . . .'

Hedda refrained from telling him that he might not live long enough to finish counting let alone enjoy the benefits of it in retirement, and passed by with no more than a smile to her private quarters. She had plans to make.

Doc Munday tended a seemingly endless stream of men to his surgery all suffering the same sickness in a variety of guises. But hangovers, in whatever gripe or groan they came, received short shrift at his hands. 'Go take a bath,' he advised bluntly, 'and stay clear of the Garter.' He suspected, however, that he was wasting his time in every case. They would all be back again tomorrow — if there was going to be a tomorrow.

Jim Squire and Jess Morden sought out Lately Poole at the barber's shop and, once the last customer had been shaved and snipped to satisfaction, paid up and left, told him of Marshal Brand's reckoning and outlined their plan to recruit an armed force of regular town men to uphold civil order. 'Minute we get wind of Lovell's men ridin' in, we move, tight as an army, fast and sure. And under orders.'

'Whose orders?' Lately had asked.

'Why, the marshal's, of course. He's in real charge round here, ain't he?'

But was he, Brand had wondered, making his slow way through the crowd to the sheriff's office?

He had arrived in a town in the grip of hanging fever; where both men and women, young and old, were obsessed with the spectacle of a notorious gunman being brought to justice. And probably obsessed more with the romance of it all as the grim reality.

Except that now, of course, if his instinctive reactions and reckoning were to be believed, the reality was itself a romance, an elaborate dupe whereby Jude Lovell would once again — as he had throughout his professional criminal life — be the only winner in town.

So just who was in charge of the events that were about to unfold — Marshal Lyle Brand, or the man being held under lock and key in Sheriff McConnell's cells?

Brand grunted to himself, dodged another swarm of back-slapping, closed his ears to the comments of the throng surrounding him and the offers of free drinks, and pushed his way through to the boardwalk fronting the sheriff's office and disappeared inside.

An ashen-faced, tired eyed deputy greeted him. 'Mornin', Marshal. Hell, this town sure gets lively early. Does it ever sleep?'

'Probably not,' grinned Brand. 'The prisoner awake?'

'He don't never seem to sleep neither. You want to see him?'

'Time I renewed our acquaintance, I reckon,' said Brand. 'Been some while.'

The deputy jangled a ring of keys and led the way to the cells.

10

'Well, well, Marshal Brand. Took your time, didn't you? I been expectin' you since long back. But, no, I'm forgettin' you've been busy, ain't you? Made a mess of my good friend, Mr Mooney, I hear. Fool . . . always was slow on the trigger when he'd been boozin'. So who've you got lined up next? Me, by any chance?'

The clipped, tight-lipped tone of arrogance in Jude Lovell's voice, the smug expression of his own assumed authority, the twinkle of sheer defiance in his eyes, all were known to Marshal Brand. He had heard the tone before, watched the sneering, condescending expression on his face, and seen that twinkle flare to the gleam of cruel death, many times. There was nothing new about Jude Lovell — the pock-pitted skin, the sweat-varnished tan, the stare, the easy hands, the loose, casual limbs — only the setting to his presence was different. Lovell had never been penned until now.

Brand waited for his eyes to adjust to the gloom and shadows of the jail area before fixing his gaze on Lovell seated in the far corner of his cell. 'Careless, wasn't it, you gettin' taken like you did?' he said slowly.

Lovell shrugged dismissively. 'Gettin' older, I guess. Them bounty boys ain't no more than kids. They got lucky.'

Lovell's eyes narrowed as he watched Brand walk thoughtfully to the left, then to the right, pause, contemplate, grunt quietly. 'Why alone out there?' asked the marshal. 'T'ain't like you to ride single-handed.' He watched while Lovell stayed silent. 'And with so many of your old friends happenin' to be so close at that. Well, they must've been. Ben Pullman, Matt Michaels, Colorado Jack, Joe Doone and, o'course, Mooney, savin' he got lead happy. You've even got the Dealer here? Why? We havin' some kinda scumbag's hoedown or somethin'? Or are they here for the wake, Jude?'

Brand permitted a half-smile, held it for a moment, then let it fade as his gaze darkened. Lovell stayed silent. 'You're goin' to hang, Jude, you know that, don't you?' said Brand quietly.

'I hear that's the plannin' of it,' grinned Lovell, 'and it's nice to have friends about at a time like this, not to mention Judge Whinnie travellin' in. And, o'course, you're here. Nothin' but the best, eh?' The grin broadened. 'Ain't you about due to retire, Mr Brand? Must be. And to think, all them good years you've spent chasin' me. Towns from here to the San Diando border; far north as Montana snows; east and west . . . and here we are in little old Saracen. I guess you deserve that retirement.'

Brand fixed the man's stare, grunted again and turned to head back to the office.

' 'Course, I ain't dead yet, Marshal,'

called Lovell. 'So you can't hang up them guns, can you? Not quite . . . not yet.'

Brand left with Lovell's laughter ringing in his ears.

★　★　★

But Brand was right. He knew it, could sense it, and he was sure he had seen just the flicker of uncertainty in Lovell's face when he had reeled off the names of the gunman's old friends.

Jude Lovell, his gang, the men gathered in the foothills of the Bigbones, and who could say how many more, were involved, working together in what was going to go down as one of the biggest bank raids in the history of the territory if not the country.

But how, in the time available and in a town as frenetic as Saracen, could it be stopped? Hang Lovell now? Have Milton Boyd clear the bank of all its monies? And hide them where? Send for help? Rally the local folk in a force to defend the town? Hell, thought Brand, he was only a step away from wallowing in a bloodbath.

He hurried from the sheriff's office as fast as the still thronging, noisy crowds would permit. He dodged into a side alley, halted, caught his breath and decided he would make for the back entrance to the Garter saloon. Maybe those so-called bounty hunters had something they might be persuaded to share with him.

Brand moved on, picking his way through the back-of-business clutter of crates, timbers, boxes, barrels and the day-to-day flotsam of booming trade. No one seemed to notice. The milling street crowd had switched its attention from him to the more colourful attractions of a bar girl on the boardwalk fronting the Garter saloon.

'Here we are, fellas!' she shouted, flouncing the layers of her dress high above her knees. 'Step right this way. You won't be disappointed!'

'You got it, gal! I'm a-comin' . . . '

whooped an old-timer, falling flat on his face in the stampede to the 'wings.

'She's all mine,' yelled a youth, climbing over the shoulders of the man in front of him.

'Not yet she ain't!' shouted another, throwing his hat high into the dusty air.

Charlton Folde bustled the girl aside and raised his arms to the oncoming rush. 'Easy now, fellas, easy. We've got gals of all natures, all sorts, all for your delight. And let me tell you — '

'No need for you to tell us anythin', mister,' boomed an ox of a man with a crimson face and throbbing neck veins. 'Just get the drinks lined up and the girls along of 'em!'

Voices whooped; some men set up a shrill cacophony of whistling. Somewhere deep in the street a window shattered, a door banged, a woman screamed then giggled, a dog barked.

Sheriff McConnell elbowed his way through the now clamouring mob. 'Hold it, will you!' he yelled, shoving aside a man with one flat punch of his clenched fist. 'Hold it, f'Chris'sake. This is my town. We do things my way, and I ain't for takin' . . . '

Another man sprawled across the dirt; a youth reached for a Colt, only to have McConnell kick it from his grip the second it left the holster. 'And there'll be none of that either.' He swung a desperate punch, more in frustration than with purpose, and felled a man trying, against the impossible odds of the throng, to light a cheroot. 'Sorry,' grunted the sheriff, and pushed on.

The bar girl continued to swirl and twirl on the boardwalk; a second girl joined her, then a third. Charlton Folde waved his arms but was fast losing control as girls poured through the 'wings like a swarm of flapping birds, skirts swinging, swirling, lifting like curtains to reveal flashes of flesh.

'Oh, my god, what in the name of sanity have we here?' groaned Jim Squire, staggering from his store ahead of a clucking, tut-tutting group of town women.

'A disgrace . . . '

'An insult . . . '

'It's retribution . . . '

'It's the end. The Good Lord giveth and sure as damnation taketh away — 'specially when it's bar whores rustling up business like it was a spring round-up!'

Milton Boyd emerged from his bank, a cigar clamped between his teeth, sweat marks staining his jacket, a shivering clerk at his side. 'For Chris'sake get a grip there, McConnell,' yelled the president losing his grip on the cigar and then cursing as the glowing sparks of the butt burned a hole in his pants.

Lately Poole left a lathered man in the chair, locked the door to his shop and took refuge in a mound of old crates behind the premises. 'There'll be a discount,' he shouted back to the abandoned customer.

The crowd continued to whoop, whistle, jeer and press forward to the saloon. Men grabbed at shirts, the seats of pants, anything, ahead of them. Dust and dirt lifted in a thickening yellow-grey haze. A man fell head first into the water trough and surfaced with an unopened bottle of whiskey clutched in his hand. The ladies outside Squire's mercantile gathered in an indignant clutch of lavender and lace and dabbed at their cheeks with already wet kerchiefs.

A shot rang out.

A silence fell as if dropped.

Voices were muffled, scrambling limbs stilled.

No one moved. No one dared to say a word.

Hedda Folde stepped from the saloon into the full glare of the sunlight, a smoking gun clutched in her right hand, and gazed over the faces of the crowd like a hen vulture assessing the choice of morsels to feed her chicks.

'Fools!' she snapped, her voice as clipped and dry as creek dirt. 'Hold it right there, the lot of you.' She scanned the mob as if about to whiplash every last man, then flashed defiance and her authority on the bar girls. 'Get back inside. I'll deal with you later.' Her eyes seemed to spit flame as they settled on her husband. 'Inside,' she ordered, and Charlton Folde went without another murmur.

'Guess we know who's wearin' the pants at the Garter, eh, boys!' jeered the old-timer dusting dirt from his battered hat.

Some men cheered their agreement, some smiled but stayed silent. Most stayed silent.

Marshal Brand had halted among the clutter and flotsam, listened for a moment to the excited mob, then eased his way back to the street in time to see Hedda Folde fire the single shot and take control of the boardwalk. But now what, he wondered? Surely she would not be so foolish as to warn the throng of the threat of Lovell's men. If word got out . . .

But his thoughts were broken by the sudden appearance at the head of the street of Jess Morden coming at some pace from the livery. The marshal swallowed quickly and felt a line of cold sweat bead in his neck. Jess had volunteered at the meeting in the bank to be the lookout for approaching riders. 'You can see clear through to the mountains from my place,' he had said. 'Anybody leaves them hills, I'll know about it.'

Brand began to move forward, jostling and pushing men aside as he headed to cut off Morden. From the corner of his eye among the heaving sea of faces he saw McConnell do the same. Both men were chilled by the same question: Had Morden seen a dust cloud heading this way? If he had, if that was why he had left the livery . . .

The first explosion shook the ground and blew the front of the sheriff's office clean across the street.

11

Glass, timbers, splinters, papers flew through the air as if in the grip of a raging tornado. A pair of men's pants, a vest, a shattered hat, a single boot were held in the air for a moment like suspended decorations. The street mob were instantly silent, as unmoving as stone, as suddenly grey as flat morning mist. Finally, a woman screamed at the sight of a timber smeared with blood; another followed, a third, until the air thinned the sounds to haunting echoes.

'Stand back. Stand clear, all of you,' urged McConnell uselessly, as no one seemed either to hear or notice him. He pushed his way through the crowd, calling the names of his deputies before he realized in an icy coldness that they had probably all died in the explosion.

Brand elbowed his way to the sheriff's side, followed almost as quickly by Jess Morden.

'Riders comin' in,' he hissed breathlessly.

'How far away?' asked Brand, wiping his eyes against the swirling dust.

'They've just left the foothills. Be about an hour before they hit town.'

'Hell!' cursed Brand, following McConnell as he picked his way through the rubble of what had once been his office.

'Where's Lovell?' shouted a man in the crowd.

'Has the rat been sprung?' called a second, pushing himself clear of the throng. 'Is that what all this is about?'

The cry went up, 'Lovell's free! You hear that, folks, that gunslingin' scumbag is loose again!'

'For Chris'sake, we don't know that for certain,' muttered McConnell, scrambling like an animal over the debris. 'We don't know . . . '

But ten seconds later, amid the blood-splattered rubble, where two deputies and the duty turnkey had died, the sheriff was facing a truth that had once seemed impossible: Jude Lovell was free again. He had been sprung by someone right here in town under his very nose.

He gulped and swallowed deeply as his watery gaze moved slowly over the grotesquely bent and buckled bars and beds, the remnants of clothing, a boot and, protruding like a limp, dead antenna from between splintered planks, a man's arm. 'How?' he murmured, his gaze settling on a scorched tin plate, a dented mug, a broken bottle. 'Who?'

'Leave this to me,' said Doc Munday, making a slow, painful way through the charred remains.

* * *

'Bounty hunters! They did it. 'Course they did, damn their mangy skins,' cursed Scrapes Tuppence, scrambling over the debris to the sheriff's side. 'Dynamite. How the hell did they get dynamite? They sure as hell didn't have it when I clapped eyes on 'em. So how come?' He wiped the dripping sweat from his face and narrowed his gaze on the sheriff's drawn face. 'You lose many?'

'Matt Stevens, Herb Dolby, Manny Loames,' muttered McConnell. He spat. 'When I get my hands on them rats — '

'Easy there, easy,' said Brand, clapping a flat hand on the sheriff's shoulder. 'This ain't the time, and this ain't the place.' He tightened his grip on the shoulder. 'Get busy. Round up all the reliable men you can, then clear the street, though I've a fancy there'll be some pullin' out pretty soon. And get Boyd to lock that bank like his life depends on it — which it probably does, anyhow.'

He turned to Jess Morden. 'Back to the livery for you and me. We'll be watching that dust-cloud like hawks.'

'But what about Lovell and them bounty hunter rats?' groaned McConnell, a nerve twitching restlessly in his drained face.

'One thing's for sure, you can bet your last dollar they ain't here in town,' said Morden. 'They'll have ridden soon as them cell walls were down. Hell, how lucky can you get?'

'Luck didn't figure in this, my friend,' clipped Brand. 'This was carefully — very carefully — planned, and we're only just gettin' started . . . '

★ ★ ★

It was a further fifteen minutes before Sheriff McConnell could bring himself to step away from the rubble that had once been his office — and darn near his whole world, if he were honest — swallow on the bitterness and hatred he felt on the death of his deputies and the turnkey, and head back to the jostle of the main street.

He was dogged and cajoled at almost every step.

'Lovell gone, Sheriff? He runnin' free?'

'Any truth in the talk them bounty

boys sprung him? How'd they manage that?'

'We hear as how there's a whole swarm of Lovell's men poundin' in.'

'That's right, straight out of the Bigbones. Goddamnit, they must've been there weeks. Mebbe months. That a fact, Mr McConnell?

'What you gonna do, Sheriff?'

'Is it safe to stay? Are we all goin' to get gunned down by Lovell's men?'

It was this last voice that brought the already jostling mob into real life.

'Well, I for one ain't stayin'. Not no how I ain't.'

'Me neither.'

'Truth of it is there ain't goin' to be no hangin'.'

'Can't hang a man when you ain't got him roped!'

Wild cheers and catcalls rang in McConnell's ears as he pushed on determinedly.

'Oh, for Heaven's sake, let 'em all go,' yelled Jim Squire from the mercantile. 'What the hell!'

The customer ladies tutted and clucked, fingered lace collars and dabbed at wet cheeks. 'Quite right, Mr Squire,' they echoed. 'Though watch the language,' the eldest cautioned.

'Don't you fret none, storekeeper,' shouted a paunchy man in a dusty derby and loud check pants, 'we'll be movin' right enough. Movin' out! And mebbe right now, eh, boys? Right now!'

'Town ain't safe!'

And those were the last three words from the mob that Sheriff McConnell heard before he stumbled on to the boardwalk fronting the bank and disappeared through the front door held open for him by Milton Boyd.

★　★　★

The door slammed shut behind him. He gulped, wiped a hand over his sweat-soaked face, blinked to bring his vision into focus, fumbled for his bandanna, but frowned and felt a sudden chill at the unnatural silence and emptiness.

Where were the clerks, the dozen or more tailored lackeys who were always either at their counters, pen-scratching diligently at leather-bound ledgers or scurrying about the place like termites? And why was the bank so gloomy, all but one of the windows shuttered, doors closed tight against the merest chink of light? Boyd was taking the security issue seriously.

'Best not take another step,' said the president at his back. 'There's a gun following your every move.'

'What the hell — ?' began McConnell, turning sharply to see Milton Boyd pressed against the door, his face flushed as if about to explode. 'What you sayin'?'

'See for yourself,' grunted Boyd.

McConnell turned again, his narrowed gaze piercing the shadowy gloom. At first there was nothing of any specific shape to see, nothing like figures or objects he might recognize. And that bothered him. Where were the staff? His mouth had started to frame the question, when a movement ahead of him, deep in shadow, rooted him to the spot. But he had seen it clear enough. The slightest shift of a gleaming gun barrel.

He swallowed, risked clearing the sweat from his face, and peered closer. 'Who . . . who's there?'

'Just ease that piece of yours clear of the holster, Sheriff, and don't say another word.'

Jude Lovell stepped from the shadow, a Colt levelled in his hand, a slow, mocking grin at his lips. The two bounty hunters flanked him, Winchesters cradled in their arms.

'Glad you could make it so soon,' said Lovell, the grin sliding to a cynical smile. His stare lingered, mocking in spite of its unblinking coldness. 'Sorry about your office. Boys here made a real mess of it, eh? Bet you weren't expectin' that!'

'You killed good men in cold blood,' croaked McConnell, the sweat beading freely on his face.

'I'm sure they were *good men* like you say.' Lovell's smile twitched. 'They're all good men, ain't they, Sheriff, till they get in the way? Then they have to die; leastways they do in my book.'

'You'll hang for that, sure as sun-up.'

'You can forget any hangin', McConnell. Hangin's are clean out of season! But the promise of one — mine to be precise — sure as hell brought the folks out, eh? You bet. Scores of 'em. Hundreds of 'em packin' the town to the very last sleepin' place. I wager business has never been so good, 'specially here at the bank.'

'You planned all this,' croaked McConnell again, his throat as rough as gravel dirt.

''Course I planned it, down to the last detail.' Lovell twirled the Colt through his fingers, watched it come to rest again then turned his attention to Milton Boyd still sweating and threatening to explode in his anger. 'Know somethin', Sheriff,' Lovell continued, 'our bank president here tells me that takin's have been — what was the word he used — yeah, that was it, phenomenal, he said, best ever. And do you know how much there is lyin' in this bank right now, every cent of it contributed as a result of my presence in your town? Any notion? Make a guess?'

McConnell shook his head, his eyes suddenly glazed and aching.

'I'll tell you,' smiled Lovell. 'One hundred thousand dollars plus, and it's all mine or will be the minute my boys ride in.' He glanced at the bank's clock. 'Which by my reckonin' won't be a deal more than thirty minutes hence. So there we are. You are about to witness one of the biggest raids ever attempted. And there ain't a thing you or that agein' Marshal Brand or Judge Whinnie or anybody else can do about it. Town's emptyin' fast and the money's all mine for the takin'.'

Lovell's smile eased from his lips. 'Relax, Sheriff,' he said quietly. 'You ain't goin' to feel a thing — not until I kill you.'

12

The dust cloud out of the Bigbones had swollen like a threatening growth. It had begun as a slow, drifting smudge, no more than might have been mistaken for a whipped up swirl of sand caught in the down draughts through the foothills.

But Jess Morden's eye knew a whole sight better. He had spent most of his working life living with the mountain range on the far horizon beyond the livery. He knew the Bigbones' moods, their twists and turns on the whims of the weather as well as the print of his own hand. And what he had seen that morning had been no freak turn of the weather. He had seen riders hell-bent on the trail to Saracen.

'Pace has slowed a mite,' he observed, his right hand shading his eyes.

'You figure that significant?' asked

Marshal Brand at his side.

'Checkin' out last-minute details on the hoof,' murmured Jess. 'They'll be here in a half-hour.'

Brand grunted, turned his back on the open land to the mountains and gazed into the still emptying town. 'Ain't wastin' any time, are they? Bailin' out faster than rats.'

'Can't say I blame 'em,' said Jess. 'This whole place could be a graveyard before sundown. Ain't much goin' to stand in Lovell's way now, is there? All them guns ridin' in. Frightenin'.' He lowered his hand from his brow. 'Mebbe we should all make a run for it.'

'That include yourself?'

The livery owner shrugged. 'Nowhere to run to, Marshal. 'Sides, I've spent my whole life here. My life *is* here. I ain't for desertin' it. Always planned on endin' my days here, anyhow. Mebbe they're comin' just that bit sooner.'

'Same go for the others, you reckon?'

Jess thought for a moment. 'I guess

so. Jim Squire's given his life to that store of his. Same goes for Lately and his barberin'. Can't speak for the Foldes. Charlton's a chancer. Risk his last dollar if he can see the chance to double it. As for that wife of his . . . hell, who's to say? Not me! As for Sheriff McConnell, well, what's he to do: stand by his badge and duty to the town, or bolt like a jack-rabbit for the nearest hole?'

'He'll stay,' said Brand.

'My thinkin' too.' Jess raised his hand to shield his eyes again. 'Meantime, where's Lovell, where's them bounty hunters, and where, in God's name is Judge Whinnie?' He sighed, and narrowed his eyes against the glare. 'Whole thing's like somethin' out of a nightmare, and darned if I can see any way out for any of us. I mean, just how . . . ' He lowered his hand, conscious now of being alone.

And he was. Marshal Brand had slipped away with all the silence of a shadow.

'You mean he pulled out, just like that at a time like this? Hell, if that ain't salt in the wound.' Jim Squire removed his hat, wafted it across his sweating face and focused again on the dust cloud. 'Where's he gone, f'Chris'sake? You ain't sayin' as how he's ridin' out?'

'Horse's gone, same as darned near all of 'em have gone, but I didn't see or hear nothin' of Brand,' said Jess, still scanning the progress of the dust cloud. 'He never said nothin'. Just disappeared.'

The storekeeper wafted his hat again, welcoming the rush of air even though it was hot and sticky. 'So we're on our own, eh? Well, ain't that all buckskin dandy!'

'Where's McConnell?' asked Jess. 'You seen anythin' of him?'

Squire frowned. 'Must still be with Boyd sealin' up the bank for what that's worth.' He replaced his hat with a defiant push. 'Goddamnit, there ain't nothin' we can do. Not a thing. No point now in tryin' to get a town force together. Could hardly raise a handful of willin' men. Best thing we can do is stay quiet and just hope Lovell spares our lives.'

'You think he will?'

Squire turned a tired but still anxious gaze on Jess. 'No — no, I don't, if I'm honest. I don't reckon he'll want to. He and his rabble will clear the bank, take whatever else they want from wherever they can get it — and leave as few witnesses as possible.' He swallowed. 'Mebbe we should follow the marshal and ride,' he added softly.

'I ain't leavin',' said Jess. 'Too much at stake here. Too much still to do. And 'sides, I want to see just what it is we got headin' in.'

'You may not be around too long to see it,' said Squire grimly, then turned at the sound of Doc Munday hurrying towards them along the dusty street, hat in one hand, bandanna swirling in the other.

'Sonofa-goddamn-bitch,' spluttered Doc,

spitting dirt, swishing the bandanna round his neck and thudding the hat against his thigh, 'I'm figurin' for this town bein' plain doomed, darned if I ain't.' He spat noisily. 'Lovell ain't left. He's right here, along of them two-faced bounty critters.' He spat again. 'He's taken the bank! That's right, just walked in and taken it.'

'How do you know?' frowned the storekeeper.

'Just been speakin' to one of Boyd's clerks. Lovell let the staff go — for now — but held Boyd. Then, when the place was all locked up and sealed, McConnell arrives, so he grabbed him too. Tell me if that ain't bein' doomed! Now all Lovell's got to do is sit tight till them rats of his out there ride in. And by the look of it, he ain't goin' to have long to wait.'

* * *

They came in a slow, dust-clouded line, fifteen to twenty strong where they could be counted in the swirling blur. Grim riders, thought Doc, easing the grip of his collar; dark-clothed, sweat-stained, mean-eyed and silent. Each man carried a rifle in addition to his packed sidearms; all rode tall and straight. Disciplined men, he reckoned; men of action who would respond instantly to an order. They would ask no questions. There would be no messing. And no conscience to live with when the deed was done. They lived in shadow and reached Saracen on that heat-soaked, sunlit day like a deep black cloud.

Jess Morden was the first to spot the odd man out when they were still some distance away.

'Who the hell's that?' he murmured, his eyes squinting against the shimmering glare. 'That who I think it is?'

'That can only be Judge Whinnie,' said Squire, mopping his face.

'The judge it surely is,' confirmed Doc. 'Only he would be sportin' a full-brimmed derby and winged collar.'

'So what happened to the stage?' grunted Jess.

No one answered. All they could do was watch.

It was another fifteen minutes before the line slowed to a steady canter and finally halted like a turning tide within sight and sound of Jess, Doc Munday and Jim Squire.

Ben Pullman and Colorado Jack eased their mounts a few steps forward. 'You some sort of welcomin' party?' asked Pullman, spitting clear of his mount's neck. 'Where's that two-bit marshal? Where's Lovell? This town clear, or you want we should do it?'

'One thing at a time,' said Squire, adjusting his coat importantly. 'Marshal Brand ain't here. He's ridden out. And don't ask me where, 'cus I ain't got a notion. He just didn't say.' His gaze tightened, wet and bloodshot. 'As for Lovell, he's where you'd expected him to be all along, ever since you and him and Lord knows how many others first plotted this thing. As for the town bein'

111

clear, sure it is — again, just like you planned, sight-seein' folk here for the hangin' have hightailed it. They ain't got no stomach for the likes of you, mister, and them dirt-swillin' ragbag you're ridin' with.' He grinned with almost a sneer. 'But they sure as biscuits left their money in the bank. And that's where Lovell is, countin' it out along of the bounty-huntin' rattlers he got to start this whole bloody shebang. So why don't you go give him a hand and then ride out of here — fast! We ain't goin' to stop you, are we? Not a handful of old Saracen townfolk. Go head. Get to it. Why waste time?'

Jim Squire's voice sank deep into his dusty throat. He mopped his face feverishly, trembled and shook at the knees. Doc Munday placed a comforting arm across his shoulders.

'He always go on like that?' clipped Colorado Jack, chewing on a wedge of tobacco. 'Such lippin' could get to seriously irritatin' a fella.'

'Now, now, don't you fret yourself, mister,' soothed Doc Munday quickly. He glanced anxiously at Jess, then smiled at the riders facing him. 'Heck, we're all a mite worked up here, ain't we, what with everythin' and this infernal heat? Gets to you. Ain't that so?'

'You can cut the smooth talkin', Doc,' flared Squire again. 'Scum of this type ain't for listenin' to decent folk. In fact, decency don't figure in their reckonin'. They wouldn't know the meanin' of the word.' The storekeeper's eyes bulged in an angry stare.

'Easy, Jim, easy,' counselled Jess, conscious of an eerie silence among the watching riders.

'Damned if I will,' said Squire, stiffening. 'Time somebody said somethin' about what's goin' on in this town, what we've been dragged down to. And don't go foolin' yourselves that Lovell and this rabble of thieves and robbers are goin' to leave us standin', let alone breathin' when they've had their fill of us and there ain't nothin' left save the dirt.' He spat. 'And now I see they've got Judge Whinnie there! Well, of course they have. Wouldn't have figured no other. What do you reckon they did, Doc? How'd they get their hands on the judge? I'll tell you. They hijacked the stage, murdered every livin' soul in sight save Judge Whinnie, and torched what was left.' His gaze froze into Pullman's face. 'You did, didn't you, mister? You murdered, plundered and doubtless raped if there were women aboard. That's what you did, and that's what you'll keep on doin' — '

And then the gun raged.

13

Jim Squire never uttered another word. He barely made a sound under the sudden blaze of Pullman's levelled Winchester. He might have seen the glint of the barrel as the rifle steadied for the shot; the look in the gunman's eyes, darkening for the kill. The roar when it came seemed to last only seconds until it climbed and floated to an echo above the jangle of tack, creak of leather as startled horses snorted, backed and came to rein again. The line of gunmen stayed silent, watching the body sprawl and twitch for the last time in the baking street dirt.

'My God,' hissed Doc, stepping forward instinctively. He dropped to one knee at Squire's side.

'He's dead, you can bet to that,' sneered Colorado Jack. 'My friend here don't miss them sorta shots, eh Ben?'

'Shut your mouth,' snapped Pullman.

'This how it's goin' to be?' said Jess, the sweat bubbling on his brow, trickling down his cheeks in dirt-streaked lines. 'Just killin' when somethin' don't suit? That how you fellas work?'

'Stand aside there, fella,' ordered Pullman, menacing the Winchester at Morden's gut. 'Don't mess where you ain't involved, otherwise . . . Otherwise it'll be *just* like this.' He reined his horse round to face the line of men. 'We're movin' in. We take the town. Any resistance, shoot. Leave the bank and the judge to me.' He swung round again to Jess and Doc. 'Get that body off the street. And you, blacksmith, make ready to stable my men's horses.'

'For how long?' asked Jess.

Pullman grinned cynically. 'As long as it takes,' he spat.

★　★　★

'But think of the money, my dear. Think of it . . . All those men, ridden in

116

from God knows where. Hot, thirsty, lookin' for some friendly relaxation. I mean, think of it.'

Hedda Folde rose slowly from the table in her private room at the Garter saloon, stared for a moment at her husband, winced inwardly at the patronizing smile on his hot, sticky face, and crossed carefully to the window overlooking the street. She watched the newly arrived riders in town continue their systematic search of the place under the shouted orders of Colorado Jack.

'You do understand what I'm sayin', don't you, my dear?' urged Folde moving closer to her, one hand reaching tentatively for her waist. 'There's money here, big money, and we, my dear, can help ourselves to more than a fair share of it. And all in a matter of days . . . hours, when I come to reckon it. Do you realize, we could be out of here, out of the dust and dirt, free of all this scumbag custom and headin' east, just like you've always wanted in under a week?' His hand settled on her waist. 'Think of it.'

Hedda made no movement. She stayed silent, watching the street, the activity, swirls of dust, flash of sunlight on gun barrels, the gleam of sweat on tight, concentrated faces. Ugly faces. Mean and impassive.

'They shot Jim Squire,' she murmured without turning.

'It happens with these types,' said Folde quickly. 'You know that. You've seen it before. As I hear it, if Squire had kept his mouth shut . . . '

'They'll shoot McConnell,' she murmured again, her gaze fixed and unblinking.

'McConnell's his own fool,' snapped Folde. 'Walkin' into that bank was as good as shootin' himself in the foot. He should've figured Lovell was there. Where else would he be, f'Chris'sake? That Marshal Brand should've warned him. Hell, he's *marshal*! And where is he now? I'll tell you: he's out of it. He's gone. Ridden out. Judge Whinnie'll have somethin' to say about that — assumin' Lovell lets him live long enough to say anythin'! And judgin' by the way this whole thing's been organized — from them bogus bounty hunters to Lovell's escape and havin' all them fellas ready and waitin' in the hills — judgin' things that way, I wouldn't give a leakin' barrel for the judge's life.' His hand tightened on Hedda's waist and he pressed himself closer. 'But none of that's goin' to trouble us, my dear. Trust me.'

The woman swung round, her eyes blazing. 'Is that all you can think of — making money out of a town on its knees?' She stiffened, her fists clenching until the knuckles whitened. 'The folk out there have been a whole sight more than our customers, they've been our friends. And now some of them, all too many, are going to get killed, shot down in cold blood for no good reason save Jude Lovell's greed. And there'll be our girls included among the bodies by the time them scum out there have finished with them. You going to stand by and watch that just so's you can pocket the money — if the rats pay, which I very much doubt? Well, are you?'

Folde's mouth opened, but a vicious well-aimed slap across his cheek silenced him before the words were given the breath to form.

'Louse!' sneered Hedda. She gathered her skirts, brushed defiantly past her husband to the table, opened a drawer at its head and took out a Colt. 'Well, I'm not — not by a long way.' She steadied the gun and levelled it. 'And make no mistake, mister, I ain't going to be one bit fussed who the hell I shoot — not if he ain't with me.'

* * *

'Let me make it perfectly clear, once and once only, so's you all know just what you and those along of you are gettin' into.' Judge Whinnie smothered his face for a moment in a large white bandanna, blinked, took a deep breath and gazed in his stoniest judge's pose over those watching him.

A stream of shafted sunlight poured through the bank's one unshuttered window. The silence in the gloomy interior seemed deeper than the blur of noise coming from the main street. The faces were wet with sweat and, save for that of Jude Lovell, tensed and tight. No one moved. No one seemed to be breathing.

The judge cleared his throat officiously and settled the gaze on Ben Pullman. 'You, mister, are in a heap of trouble: bushwhackin' a stage of the line, destroyin' it; murderin' the passengers, driver and shotgun; kidnappin' myself, the circuit judge . . . and all this on top of what I am sure is an already long and impressive list of law-breakin' activities.' He grunted. 'You and a dozen more will hang.'

The gaze swung to take in the man known only as the Dealer, then Matt Michaels and Joe Doone. 'Same goes for you,' said Whinnie. 'You were all there, all a part of what happened. I know. I, too, was there. Remember?' He grunted again, let his gaze wander over Sheriff McConnell and Milton Boyd and come to rest on Jude Lovell.

'Save your breath,' grinned Lovell. 'I ain't interested. And just in case you were wonderin', my hangin' ain't takin' place.' He strolled casually towards the locked doors. 'I've been generous to you, Judge. I've kept you alive; you've had your little say, your moment of *presidin'* . . . ' He swung round sharply. 'But now it's over. Enough. From here on you do exactly as ordered when you're ordered. One mess up, and you're dead. As it is, you'll live for just as long as I say you will. Same goes for the sheriff here and Boyd — and anybody else I see fit to dispose of. You understand?'

Judge Whinnie's chest expanded under an angry intake of breath. His face disappeared again behind the bandanna.

Milton Boyd fumed silently but was

already feeling the first chill of fear.

McConnell's eyes narrowed. His thoughts struggled for any proper shape and priority. How the hell was he going to break out of the bank? Damn it, he had a town to run. Had he? Was there still a town out there? Where was Marshal Brand? Had somebody — perhaps the marshal himself — ridden out to raise help? What were Lovell's plans? Were they all going to die?

'Get the vaults opened. Get some of the boys in here to start loadin'. Post guards. Seal the town tight. Nobody rides in. Nobody rides out. Shoot any fool who tries.' Lovell twirled a Colt through his fingers. 'Let's move. We work through the night. No shirkin'.' He gave the Colt a final spin and holstered it with a thud. 'Time's money, and there's a lot of it!'

14

A strange, locked-in stillness tightened its grip on Saracen as that day wore on painfully. The once bustling, noisy street, where the talk had been of only one thing, the hanging of Jude Lovell, lay empty, silent, suddenly remote as if standing back from time.

Only a handful of town men patronized the Garter under the watchful gaze of a half-dozen of Lovell's men. Colorado Jack prowled the street, the back alleys, businesses and empty buildings like a hungry lion in search of a meal, his eyes probing, his senses alert to every sound, every movement. The gunslingers following him helped themselves to whatever took their fancy, wherever they found it.

Lately Poole touted hopefully for business. 'Hot baths at a reasonable rate, fellas. Clean towels. No second users. And I got some decent specials from back East. Guaranteed to fetch the women. Dollar a splash, or free with the shave and cut.' But business on that day was slow. Lovell's boys regarded water for washing as a waste, and needed no inducement to attract women. They simply took them.

Charlton Folde's day had gone from bad to worse and showed no signs of reversing. He had been disappointed, not to say stunned, at his wife's reaction to the prospect of fast profits from Lovell and his men. Now, watching over a three-quarters empty bar and a pale, dispirited clutch of bar girls at a corner table, he was beginning to wonder if pulling out overnight with the cash he already had stashed in his personal safe might be the smartest move.

After all, everybody knew or could guess what was happening at the bank. Heck, there were enough roughneck gunmen guarding the place at every door and window to signal Lovell's intent without a word being said.

Trouble was, what would happen when Lovell was ready to ride? How many would he leave breathing? Would he garnish his bank spoils by taking what he wanted of the town? Would he turn his boys loose, give them free rein to do as they wished? Or maybe he would simply torch the place and watch it burn from some place safe in the Bigbones?

One thing was for certain, reckoned Folde as he watched a gunslinger help himself to a second free bottle of whiskey, there would be no help on its way from another town. There was no time. And as for Marshal Brand . . . The law had been blown clear of Saracen on the first puff of the Lovell breeze!

Shame of it was that Sheriff McConnell stood alone without a hope of changing the situation. And as for Judge Whinnie, who would give a tin mug for his chances?

So, pulling out while the going was at least on level ground might not be such a bad idea. There was and could be a tempting future out there for a man of vision and an eye to the keen profit.

With or without a wife.

* * *

Hedda Folde stood stripped naked in the shadowy gloom of her private room. She had shed every last item of her expensive, lavishly cut and tailored eastern clothes. Every trinket had been thrown aside. Her long dark hair had been released from its coiffured tightness to hang loose and free across her shoulders. She relaxed, smiled softly to herself and poured a stiff measure of whiskey from a bottle on the table in front of her.

For the first time in more years than she cared to recall she felt a sense of freedom, of discarding an old life for the new. And this was the beginning.

She finished the drink, replaced the glass, smiled again and stood for a moment listening to the sounds around her. The bar was quiet — too quiet by half for her husband's liking — but the street beyond still carried the soft drone of comings and goings, the occasional bang of a door, heavier footfalls across the boardwalk, snort of a hitched mount, sound of a man's voice.

How much longer, she wondered, before Lovell made his next move? How many hours still left before the killing began?

She turned to the new set of clothes arranged on her bed and began to dress quickly. Maybe there was not so much time; maybe it would all happen sooner than anyone expected. She needed to move — fast but efficiently if her plans were going to work and she stayed a step ahead of Lovell, not to mention her husband.

She hesitated and felt the soft chill of cold sweat in her neck at the sudden tap on the door.

'Whoever it is I ain't half decent,' she called. 'Come back later.'

'I'm not for waitin', ma'am,' came a

flat, dull voice from the other side of the door. 'I ain't got the time.'

'Who is that?' frowned Hedda, struggling to adjust the belt on her trousers.

'Name's Michaels, ma'am. Matt Michaels. One of Lovell's men.'

★　★　★

Jess Morden held the white-hot shoe in the jaws of the iron tongs for a moment, examined it through narrowed eyes, then plunged it into the tub of water at his side. The resulting hiss and clamour of steam suited his mood. Like the shoe, his anger, not to mention his frustration, was white hot. But unlike his handiwork, there was no place and nothing to plunge himself into to cool off.

'You sure as Sunday looked like you meant that,' said Lately Poole from his seat on a straw bale a safe distance from the raging forge.

'I did,' said Jess, examining the shoe

again before tossing it to an already growing pile. 'Just wish I could . . . Hell, what's the use? We're like hens in a coop, and there ain't no way out. Not that I can see, anyhow.'

'Mebbe that lawman, Marshal Brand, will bring some help,' said Lately, selecting a straw to chew on. 'Hell, I can't believe he's just hightailed it out of here. Lawmen don't do that, do they?'

'Looks a whole lot likely this one has.' Jess drew a roughly shod shoe from a second pile, fired it and struck his hammer across it, imagining for a second that it might have been the head of any one of Lovell's men. 'Or mebbe he was gettin' too old. I heard say as how he's due to retire. Perhaps this was his last job.' Jess wielded the hammer. 'Huh,' he sweated, 'some job he made of it!'

Lately chewed on the straw for a while as his gaze swept over the near deserted street, paused briefly at the still heavily guarded bank before settling on a group of Lovell's men making their way to the saloon.

The men had disappeared through the batwings when he spoke again. 'Mebbe I should salvage what I can from the shop and pull out. Mebbe you should too. Damnit, it's lookin' to be as how the only fate we have is the same as hit Jim Squire, God rest his soul.'

'I ain't for leavin',' said Jess. 'Said so before, sayin' it now. 'Sides, I got a stableful of horses to tend. They ain't harmed nobody, and it sure ain't their fault they're here.' He fired the rough shoe again and attacked it with the brute force of the hammer. 'All I'm lookin' for,' he hissed, through a succession of blows, 'is some way — any way — of stoppin' Lovell before he heads for them mountains never to be sniffed again. You got any ideas?'

Lately threw aside the straw and slid from the bale to his feet. 'Just one,' he began. 'T'ain't much, but it occurred to me — '

Two fast shots rang out with a roar that seemed to split the sultry air.

'They came from the saloon,' gulped Lately, sweat beading like bubbles across his brow.

'Too right they did,' croaked Jess, throwing the hammer to the ground. 'Come on!'

★ ★ ★

The door to Hedda Folde's private room at the saloon had burst open before the dull echo of the second shot had faded.

Colorado Jack was ahead of the handful of men who stared in silence at the scene before them.

Hedda Folde stood with her back to the window, a wisp of smoke curling softly from the barrel of the Colt clutched in her hand. Her shirt had been ripped from her shoulders. A slow trickle of blood deepened in the cleavage of her breasts. She seemed unaware of the sudden clutter of men filling the room and deaf to the sounds of their murmurs, the noises in the bar, the scrape and thud of footfalls as more men approached. Like those already close enough, she could only stare at the body of Matt Michaels sprawled at the foot of the bed.

'Is he dead?' asked a bewildered voice.

Nobody answered.

'She shoot him?' gulped a town man raising himself on tiptoes to see over the heads of the others.

'What the devil . . . What's goin' on here? Where's my wife? Hedda . . . Hedda . . . ' Charlton Folde elbowed his way into the room, sweat pouring from his face to his damp, limp shirt. 'Hedda, what in hell's name have you done?'

'Should've thought that pretty obvious,' mouthed Colorado, easing his weight to one hip. 'She's killed him. Done a thorough job too by the look of it.' He grinned. 'How come, ma'am? My good friend get on your nerves? Weren't you for gettin' frisky with him? That why you shot him?'

133

The woman was a full minute before she lifted her eyes from the body and gazed without blinking into Colorado's face. 'I shot him,' she murmured. 'And you'll be joining him if you and the rest of your rabble don't get the hell out of here. Now!'

15

Doc Munday trickled a scoop of sand from one hand to the other, then scattered it loosely across the ground in front of him.

'As easy as that and just about as far flung,' he said, dusting the last grains from his hands. 'Them folk we had filling the street to near chokin' are all gone. Every last one of them. Far and wide. East and west. North and south. Fast as they arrived for the big spectacle, so they pulled out. And only Jude Lovell takes the payoff.'

He glanced at the men seated round him at the back of the livery forge: Jess Morgan, Lately Poole, Scrapes Tuppence, two youths and a man in a pair of baggy dungarees. 'But — and this is the point, my friends — they've all had to travel somewhere and reach a destination. And that means it ain't goin' to be long before just about the whole of the territory gets to hear of what happened in Saracen.'

'You're right, Doc,' said Scrapes, smacking his lips. 'But it ain't goin' to be a deal of use to us, is it? Time somebody, somewhere puts a posse t'gether Lovell and his rats'll be long gone. And the bank'll be empty.'

'And the street like as not full of dead bodies,' added the man in dungarees. 'Our bodies.'

'What about that marshal fella we had here?' asked one of the youths. 'Where's he?' He hooked his thumbs in his belt. 'Strikes me Mrs Folde's got a whole sight more guts than any lawman. Way she dealt with that sidekick of Lovell's was somethin' else, eh? No messin'. Bang, you're worm meat!'

'But highly dangerous if you ask me,' said Jess, raking ash clear of the forge. 'Lovell ain't goin' to take a killin' like that lyin' down.'

'Mebbe he's too busy countin' and

packin' all that money to notice,' grinned Scrapes. 'Anyhow, it don't seem Mrs Folde is one bit fussed about what she did. Fella bit off a deal more than he could chew when he tangled with her. She's tough, all through. Which is more than can be said for that husband of hers. Darn it, I reckon he'd sell his own kin if he could see a fast dollar in it.'

Lately came to his feet from the bench where he had been seated and gazed back down the street to the silent saloon and the monotonous patrol of the men guarding the bank.

'Can't be long now before they're all through there,' he said quietly. 'Mebbe we should keep a closer watch for McConnell. God, if them scum get to killin' him . . .'

'Don't let's paint any darker pictures than we've already got,' urged Doc, scooping another handful of sand. 'Brutal fact of it is, that we've lost only McConnell's deputies and poor Jim Squire. That's bad enough, but it could be a whole sight worse.'

'And might still be,' mused Scrapes, blinking across his tired grey eyes. 'Take a look down the trail there. It's mebbe ridin' in right now.'

★ ★ ★

Four riders; dirty, dusty, sweat-grimed but still with smiles on their faces in spite of what seemed to those watching their arrival, a long, hot journey.

They came in on the back trail to the west of the town's sprawling street, one rarely used save by stray travellers who happened across it more by chance than design.

'Ragbag drifters,' muttered Scrapes as those gathered at the livery shielded their eyes against the late afternoon glare and watched the riders reach the far end of the street. 'Spit to a dollar they ain't a clue to what they've ridden into.'

The beat of hoofs, creak of leather, jangling tack, snorts of mounts and raised voices urging the lathered horses to a halt, brought handfuls of town folk from behind doors, windows and the deeper shadows of boardwalks and side alleys, all curious to see just who had been fool enough to ride into Saracen.

The town folk simply stared, too mindful of their own safety to open up a conversation with the strangers, and already conscious of the slow approach of Lovell's men led by Colorado Jack.

The taller of the riders eased his mount forward as the dust swirls began to settle. The man ran a hand over his smudged, tanned face from where his ice-blue eyes glinted like snow pools. 'Howdy,' he grinned, raising an arm. 'Figured on the place bein' a deal busier.' He gazed round the locked and barred stores and merchants, the scatterings of silent, watchful folk, lack of hitched mounts, the gathering line of men cradling Winchesters moving towards him.

'We're here for the hangin',' he said, tightening the rein on his restive mount. 'We too late or somethin'?'

Colorado halted the line of men. He waited; spat deliberately into the dirt, grunted and sighed. 'There ain't goin' to be no hangin',' he said, a slow, soft smile edging across his lips.

The rider tightened the rein again. 'Hell, no hangin'? You hear that boys — no hangin'.' He wiped his face of the still gleaming sweat of the ride. 'We've come a long way for the occasion,' he mouthed. 'You bet. Close on eighty miles over them western ranges. Some rough ridin' out there, mister. You bet on it. Real rough. And now no hangin'. Hell, if that ain't some blow. Ain't that so, boys?' The riders at his back nodded and murmured their agreement. 'Hell, yes, some blow,' the rider continued. 'T'ain't every day a fella gets to seein' a man like Jude Lovell kickin' at the end of a rope, eh? You can bet to that too.'

He stared hard at Colorado, then at the sidekicks flanking him; the guards still in position at the bank, the four men watching from the livery, the silent groups of town folk. 'You here for the hangin', fella?' he asked. 'You and your boys?'

'Oh, sure,' said Colorado, permitting himself a full smile as some of the sidekicks tittered quietly. 'You got it, mister. Here for the hangin', 'ceptin' it ain't goin' to happen. Not now it ain't.'

'How come? What happened here? Where have all the folk gone?'

Colorado adjusted his stance with a slow shift of weight. 'Well, now, that's a long story, mister, and I wish I had the time to tell it, but frankly — '

'Ah, no matter,' scoffed the rider with a dismissive wave of his hand. 'We'll just rest up for the night, look to the mounts and mebbe have ourselves a good time at the saloon there, then we'll push on. Town don't look to bein' a place to be if there ain't goin' to be a hangin'. No, don't you fret, mister, we'll be gone — '

'Yeah, well, we have a slight problem there,' said Colorado, shifting his

141

weight again. 'T'ain't quite as simple as you put it.'

The rider's mount snorted. 'Oh, how come?' frowned the man.

'Well, you see Mr Lovell don't exactly take to visitors to town, specially strangers. And with him bein' so busy hereabouts . . . '

'You mean to say as how Jude Lovell's here? Right here in town? Alive? But that . . . that don't make no sense if there ain't goin' to be no hangin'. No sense at all. I mean, damnit, if he's here, then the law . . . ' He checked himself sharply, swallowed, wiped a fresh beading of sweat from his brow. 'There ain't no law, is there?' he croaked. His gaze moved over the town folk again, Colorado's line of men, the silent saloon, the stiff, staring guards at the bank. 'Is there?' he gulped. 'Heard tell as how there was a marshal and a circuit judge here. There ain't nothin', nobody, is there, savin' you and them men back of you?'

'S'right,' grinned Colorado. 'Just us,

like you say. And that's how it's goin' to stay.' He signalled to the line. 'Seems like you fellas found the wrong place at the wrong time.'

And then the Winchesters blazed until there was nothing of the riders from the west that moved.

16

Doc Munday was the first to speak. 'More bodies. Dead bodies. They're all we ever get round here,' he muttered, collecting his bag before beginning the dusty walk from the livery to the crowded street. 'Guess they'll be callin' for me down there. God knows why. Dead's dead whichever way you see it.'

Scrapes Tuppence removed his hat, mopped his bald head with a spotted bandanna, and scratched his neck. 'Murder. Ain't no other word for it.'

Jess Morden pushed the rolled sleeves of his shirt to the tops of his arms. 'Goddamnit, we can't just stand here watchin' all this. Got to do somethin'.'

'Sure,' said Lately, 'and the first thing you say you'll get yourself shot up by them scum down there. Them rats ain't for bein' reasoned with, Jess. You don't

144

talk to 'em. Only thing they understand is guns — guns and the death they can wreak. And there just ain't enough of us. You want a bullet in your gut, that Colorado sonofabitch will oblige, or get one of them sidekicks to do it for him, soon as spit on you. Look at him now. He couldn't give a damn for them he's just had shot. And he won't give a damn for you neither. Stay clear. There's got to be another way.'

The man in baggy dungarees stared into the street thronged with gunmen, bewildered onlookers, nervous mounts and dead bodies. 'If there is another way, it'd better get here soon while there's still some of us still standin'.'

The youths kicked restlessly at loose dirt. 'Guns, we need guns,' murmured one of them.

Scrapes spat. 'And that ain't no reason for you young 'uns to go gettin' all hot-headed. Like Lately here says, them rats'll shoot you easy as takin' breath. I know, I've seen types like them before.'

'Yeah, yeah,' said the second youth. 'In the meantime — '

'In the meantime, Jude Lovell's puttin' in an appearance down there,' said Jess, stepping forward to focus a closer look on the street.

* * *

Jude Lovell emerged from the shuttered bank to the glow of the late afternoon like an animal stirring from its darkened lair. Ben Pullman stood to his left; Sheriff McConnell, Milton Boyd and Judge Whinnie a step ahead of the supposed bounty hunters, Chet Freeman and Lud Smith.

'Nosyin' drifters, here to see the hangin',' grinned Colorado Jack gesturing to the bodies. 'Best get the place cleaned up, eh? Ain't goin' to be no hangin'.'

'Hold it,' said Lovell, coming to the edge of the boardwalk, his presence tall and erect, his gaze as penetrating as a beam as he took in the crowd of town folk, all staring, some sweating, some pale, some intrigued, most too scared to move on.

Lovell's gaze scanned the faces as if to memorize each and every one. 'We've had a good haul here today,' he began in a voice sharpened by an edge of mockery. 'Real good. Better than I'd expected.' His grin spread to a broad smile. 'Kinda satisfyin', ain't it, when everythin' goes to plan?'

'We set for pullin' out, boss?' asked Colorado. He gazed into the skies. 'Coupla hours ridin' left if we shift now.'

'I figure not, leastways not just yet,' drawled Lovell. He adjusted the set of his hat. 'No, I reckon we should leave Saracen with somethin' else — somethin' truly fittin' — for folk to remember us by. Yeah, somethin' the whole town's been lookin' forward to for days. And I ain't of a mind to go disappointin' folk. Fact is, I'm feelin' generous. Sure, I am. I've gotten lucky this past week, so why not share it, eh?'

Lovell's smile lit up his face. The sweat gleamed and glistened on his dark stubble. A thin trickle made its slow way from beneath his hat to his cheek where it spread like an estuary. 'Let's have this hangin' Saracen's been so keen on stagin'. Why not? We'll have it tonight. At midnight.'

'Who we hangin', boss?' called a flat-nosed man from the line of sidekicks.

Another swished his dustcoat with an excited flourish. 'Yeah, that's right. Who's goin' to be the lucky critter?'

The sidekicks laughed and joked among themselves. The onlooking town folk stayed silent, huddled into board-walk shade as if hoping it would swallow them.

'F'Chris'sake, what now?' muttered Doc under his breath, conscious of Scrapes hissing through his gappy teeth.

The youths fidgeted boot caps through dirt. Jess Morden pushed at his rolled up shirt-sleeves. The man in baggy dungarees stepped back instinctively to Lately Poole's side.

Lovell took a measured stroll to the left, paused, turned and strolled back. He waited. 'I suppose,' he began thoughtfully, scratching his chin, 'I suppose we should by rights be hangin' that two-bit, old man of a marshal name of Brand, but seein' as how he seems to have hightailed it in pursuit of savin' his own miserable skin, I guess we'll have to settle for second choice.'

The sidekicks stood in silence. Colorado Jack's grin almost bubbled on his sticky face. Nobody on the crowded boardwalks dared to move. Judge Whinnie fumed and turned a deep shade of purple. McConnell and Boyd said nothing under Pullman's gloating gaze.

'And I guess,' continued Lovell, 'that brings us to Sheriff McConnell here and Judge Whinnie.' He scratched his chin again. 'Tough choice between the two of them,' he mused for a moment, the glint of one eye on his audience.

'Both represent the law, which, as you all know, I ain't much for; both of them — '

'Hang the pair of 'em and be done with it!' jeered a sidekick.

Lovell spread his arms as if in a gesture of sudden revelation. 'Of course, that's it,' he smiled. 'Hang 'em both! Should've thought of that myself. Well done, fella. That's what we'll do — hang the pair of them. Tonight. Right here in the street. Midnight. And you're all invited!'

★ ★ ★

Hedda Folde closed her ears to the saloon bar racket beyond her room and refilled the glasses of her guests.

'One thing's for certain,' said Jess Morden, taking his measure in his hand, 'Lovell won't be pullin' out 'til first light, and mebbe then some if those boys of his keep drinkin' like they are right now.'

'My husband will see to that,' scoffed

150

Hedda, pouring herself another drink. 'Charlton's vision goes no further than his own skin and right now how to save it. If that means a supply of free booze, my husband's your man!'

'But his luck might not hold,' pondered Lately Poole. 'If he reckons for one minute them scum are goin' to just ride out, he's sure as hell got another think comin'.'

'That's as maybe,' said Doc, carrying his replenished drink to the window. 'I'm a heap more concerned with how we're goin' to save McConnell and Judge Whinnie from the rope.' He consulted his silver timepiece. 'And the hours, friends, are tickin' by awful fast.'

'Don't seem to be a way, does there?' grimaced Lately. 'We could try raisin' enough guns to shoot it out with Lovell's men, but, hell, where's the sense in that if half the town folk end up dead?'

'T'ain't no use talkin' with Lovell,' said Jess. 'Even if he'd listen, we ain't in no bargainin' position. Fact is, we're about as useless as the street dirt out there.'

'And still no sign of Marshal Brand,' added Lately morosely.

Hedda drummed her fingers lightly on the polished surface of her dressing-table. 'Can't get it through my head that a fella the likes of him — lawman at that — just rode out. Hell, is that what lawmen do when they get to seeing retirement verandas and comfortable rockers?' The drumming reached a crescendo and finished. 'Didn't show no thoughts for preserving himself when he shot Frank Mooney right there in front of the batwings, did he? Heck, I'll wager he wasn't thinking of rocking in the shade when he pulled the trigger that night!'

Doc shrugged. 'All I can reckon so far as he's concerned is that somethin' must've — '

The door to the room burst open with a thrust that sent it crashing back on it hinges to the wall.

'Boss wants you. Right now,' ordered Colorado Jack.

'Do you mind?' flared Hedda. 'This happens to be — '

'I ain't standin' on no ceremony here, lady,' snapped the gunslinger, eyeing the others like a watchful hawk. 'You break up this cosy little meetin' and do like the boss says. He don't take to bein' kept waitin'. So shift!'

'What's the rat want?' spat Hedda, her unblinking gaze fixed on Colorado's face. 'He looking for another innocent victim to hang!'

'Just cut the talk, lady, before I get to losin' my own patience. And you men, get out and keep clear of trouble if you want to stay breathin'.'

'There's goin' to come a day of reckonin' for all this,' said Doc, collecting his bag. 'You just mark my words, fella, a day of reckonin'. And you ain't goin' to like it one bit. Not one bit. You hear what I'm sayin'?'

Colorado Jack stared at Doc until it seemed he would lash out. Instead, he simply smiled. 'Just count yourself lucky you ain't been selected for hangin' — yet!'

Hedda Folde stifled a shudder and left the room in stately silence.

17

Saracen waited in fear of sunset and with dread of the night to follow. The town folk had seen the drained haunted look on the faces of Sheriff McConnell and Judge Whinnie, men condemned to die at midnight on the whim of Jude Lovell. But in the sight of them, had they also seen their own futures? How many more would Lovell choose to hang? How many would die when his sidekicks' guns were turned loose? Did he intend leaving anyone alive?

Jess Morden had found himself with no time to consider the dark prospect. He had been ordered to provide a wagon and a full, fresh team of horses, 'Back of the bank right now', as the greasy-faced messenger had growled.

Doc Munday, on the other hand, had too much time to reckon on the mayhem, death and destruction that might be only hours away.

'Hell,' he had tried to reason with Charlton Folde, 'I ain't got no more influence over Lovell than yourself. Plain obvious to me why he's taken your wife — high-investment hostage, ain't she? He holds her and her life against the first man fool enough to raise a hand to threaten him. As for bargainin' with him, you do it. She's your wife and you have the money. Mebbe Lovell will sell her back to you — at the right price.'

'But we can't just leave her in that rat's hands,' the saloon proprietor had blustered under a lathering of sweat. 'Let's raise guns. Get the town men organized.'

'And you go out there into that bar of yours and try doin' it,' Doc had reasoned. 'There ain't a town man, myself included, who ain't in sympathy with your situation. Damn it, Hedda's a fine-lookin' woman and you can bet there ain't a single red-blooded male in Saracen who ain't at some time or other enjoyed her pleasures. That's fact.' He had taken a deep breath. 'Right now she's alive and, I'll wager, more than holdin' her own. And that, if you want the truth, is as good as it can be for her for now.'

Lately Poole, Scrapes Tuppence, the man in baggy dungarees and the two youths had settled themselves in the shadows of the boardwalk facing the saloon. From there, in the otherwise deserted street, they had watched the comings and goings of Lovell's men as they sought the ready booze and bewildered but still available bar girls.

'Appetites like hounds,' observed Scrapes. 'Ain't never any knowin' when they've had enough of anythin'.'

'Mebbe they'll booze themselves into stupors,' added one of the younger men.

'Yeah,' scoffed Lately, 'and I might get to barberin' on the moon!'

'Best we can do is wait,' said Scrapes. 'Things have a habit of just happenin'.'

But no one had understood what he meant.

Hedda Folde had refused to sit down. She had stood, silent, statuesque, seemingly indifferent to the activity around her, but watched every movement in the gloomy, shadow-lined bank of the loading of the money from the safes to the wagon drawn up out back.

It was a slow process she had reckoned; thorough but slow under the hawkish gaze of Lovell, Pullman and the one they called the Dealer. Nothing was being overlooked; every dollar, it seemed, accounted for. There would be no crumbs when the plate was cleared.

Milton Boyd was watching proceedings in a state of near collapse. The bank — *his* bank — was being systematically, clinically stripped bare. There would be nothing left. He would be reduced to total poverty. Not, perhaps, that it would matter. Lovell would kill him, anyway. He would be dead along of Sheriff McConnell and all the others, but not, surely, Hedda

158

Folde. They would not kill a woman in cold blood, would they?

One glimpse of the manic stare in Lovell's eyes was enough to confirm that he would.

The look in McConnell's eyes was one of hatred and defiance. He could only fume, contain his anger, fight his disappointment and wonder for the hundredth time just how he was going to get out of this miserable mess. Not only get himself out, but somehow save the town from spinning into the very flames of hell. Was there a way? Was there the time? Were there the men, the resources? Just who was going to . . .

But it was then, at the moment of McConnell's frustration, that Colorado Jack bustled his way through the working sidekicks to Lovell's side. And for the first time in hours there was a look of doubt and anxiety on the gunman's face.

In fact, he had turned a distinctly grim shade of grey.

As ever in Saracen, even in a time of crisis, the news travelled fast. And it was dramatic. Three of Lovell's men were dead; killed, silently, efficiently, by someone who knew exactly how to handle a deadly blade.

'What happened?' asked the man in dungarees, watching the sudden burst of new activity at the saloon.

'Accordin' to what Doc's just been tellin' me,' began Lately Poole, 'seems like that Colorado fella worked out some sort of rota whereby he had four men patrollin' the town, east to west, north to south, practically round-the-clock. Well, three of the critters went missin' about an hour ago. The fourth fella made it back to report to Colorado who's at the bank with Lovell right now.'

'Who'd do that?' gulped the man, his eyes widening, sweat beading on his cheeks. 'Who? One of us? One of the town men?'

'Can't figure it,' said Lately. 'Neither can Doc. I ain't heard of anybody havin' the notion to go it alone. Sure, we all feel the same, but to do that — attack one of Lovell's men, kill him and then take out two more — hell, that's callin' for real guts.'

'And a fair deal of know-how,' added Scrapes with a nod and a careful tap on the side of his nose. 'Now, for my money, that could only be — '

A sudden surge of lantern light outside the bank and the appearance in the glow of it of Lovell and a handful of his men quickly emptied the saloon and drew the folk from their homes.

He stood in silence, his shape dark and menacing, his shadow stretching like some grotesque talon, until the crowd ended their shuffling and murmuring and settled their attention on him.

'So who's bein' smart, eh?' he drawled. 'Who's gettin' above himself and fancies takin' me on?'

The street had fallen into a cold,

unreal silence where even a man's heavy breathing, the softest movement of a boot might be heard. But no man left his place on the boardwalk. No one moved. Silence thickened.

Lovell eased his weight in his arrogant stance; a shift to the left, a shift to the right. His gaze burned. Fingers drummed lightly across the butt of a holstered Colt.

He grinned. 'Well, o'course, I ain't expectin' any single one of you to step up here and tell me as how you're responsible for the killin' — the stabbin' to death this very night — of three of my men. Oh, yes, *three* men, all of 'em out here on the street. Three good men.'

Lovell relaxed his pose and walked slowly, carefully along the boardwalk, into and out of the lantern glow, stopping occasionally to stare into the crowded, fearful faces of the town folk.

'I don't hear nobody ownin' up to them killin's, and I figure I could stand here all night and still not hear a voice raised.' He grinned. 'So be it. But I reckon as recompense for them deaths I'll add another to my list of hangin's. And why not?' The grin faded. 'I'm holdin' the woman there, Hedda Folde, against any man raisin' a hand against me. And I'm takin' her with me when we pull out of this godforsaken town.'

Lovell stopped pacing. 'Seein' as how Mrs Folde won't be needin' a husband no more, we'll hang him along of the sheriff and the judge. All right? You hear that? And just so's we don't go wastin' anymore of my time we'll bring the hangin's forward. We'll get 'em over with right now while you're all so conveniently gathered.'

He turned to Pullman and Colorado Jack. 'Ten minutes. Then they hang.'

18

If it had been expected by Jude Lovell and his men that a voice might be raised that night at his announcement he was sorely mistaken. A full three minutes after he had left the boardwalk, his troupe of sidekicks in his wake as he returned to overseeing the hoard of bank money being packed and loaded, the town folk stood in the same haunted silence. Still no one moved. Still no words were uttered.

Were they walking into a nightmare, or was this it? Was the look on the face of the fellow standing next to them the expression of his personal fear, or the mirror of their own?

It was Doc Munday, Jess Morden, Lately Poole and Scrapes Tuppence who did their best to hold the line between being root scared and an outbreak of panic.

'God almighty, if some young hot-head gets to bein' bravo gun happy, this town'll run with blood,' warned Doc, as he and the others gathered in a dark huddle back of the saloon.

'Mebbe we should call a meetin',' said Lately vaguely.

'A *meetin*, f'Chris'sake,' scoffed Jess. 'Hell, we ain't got barely the time to take breath, let alone call a meetin'! Three men are goin' to die here tonight in only a matter of minutes. Lovell's goin' to hang 'em and then ride out of here with a stolen fortune and holdin' Hedda Folde as hostage. And he'll kill her soon as spit, make no mistake.' He wiped fresh sweat from his burning face. 'And there ain't a thing we can do about none of it.'

The group fell to their own silence for a moment.

'Still don't know who did them stabbin's, do we?' mused Scrapes, fingering the charred bowl of an old cherrywood. 'Nobody seen him. Nobody heard him. Town man, or an outsider?

One or the other, and my fancy would be for him to be an outsider.' He smacked his lips in anticipation of the pipe. 'Marshal Brand.'

'You figure he's here?' asked Lately.

'I figure just that,' said Scrapes. 'I don't reckon he went anywhere. He's been right here in Saracen all along.'

'Mebbe,' said Jess, 'but he's still only one man, ain't he? He's still only one gun. And one gun ain't — '

'Hold it,' hushed Doc. 'Things are happenin' out there on the street. Lovell's movin'.'

'Damnit if I ain't for takin' up my own piece and shootin' one of them devils,' cursed Lately. 'Just one. Anyone.'

'And that's all it would be,' said Doc. 'You'd be right behind him!'

The sound of voices began to fill the street. The saloon bar emptied again. Lantern lights glowed and swayed. The sidekicks jeered and jostled the three men down the street and into the deeper shadows to where ropes had been flung across the mighty limb of an ancient tree and three crates arranged beneath them. Here, the condemned men would take their last stand.

Soon they would be dead bodies whose weight at the end of the ropes would fill the night with the creaking of ghosts.

★ ★ ★

The crowd had been pushed, shoved and jostled into position by the sidekicks like a herd of sullen cattle and left to simmer in the sticky night heat before the condemned men were marched out.

Sheriff McConnell and Judge Whinnie came quietly, their hands roped behind them, their faces wet and gleaming but impassive with gazes fixed defiantly ahead. As Doc Munday muttered, 'They ain't neither of 'em givin' the rats the pleasure of anythin'.'

Not so Charlton Folde. He was under the close guard of Joe Doone and protesting and pleading his innocence every inch of the dusty way.

'Hell, so what've I done?' he blustered, stumbling under the prodding of Doone's Winchester. 'Damnit, I've shown you fellas every hospitality — and then some — so where's the beef? Just makin' me the one because of my wife, ain't you? Just that. Just so's you can have her no strings attached, eh? Well, all right, have her, do what you like with her — and you can have the business along of her if you've a mind. Sure, help yourselves. Whatever there is. Booze, money, girls. I ain't fussed. Hell, what do I care? There's always some other place to start up, ain't there?'

'Not for you there ain't,' growled Doone. 'Boss says you're for hangin', so hang you will. Best settle yourself with the thought while you got the chance.'

Folde's appeal to the town men lining the street met with blank stares and grey expressionless faces. As Scrapes Tuppence murmured, through a drift of pipe smoke, 'Like I keep sayin', he'd sell anythin' for his own skin — the rat!'

'It's goin' to happen, ain't it?' said Jess, wiping a hand across his face. 'Lovell's goin' to do it. He's goin' to hang 'em. And what then, f'Chris'sake?'

The condemned men and the side-kicks pushed on towards the ominously lantern lit tree, the noosed ropes and wooden crates where more of Lovell's men waited cradling Winchesters.

Lovell himself, with the bogus bounty hunters, Ben Pullman and Colorado Jack flanking him, brought Hedda Folde from the bank to the street as if parading her for the town to admire. She walked with the same erect detachment she had shown since being taken hostage. She looked neither to left nor right; her gaze was steady, her steps assured, the resolve almost glowing in her face. She might, dressed as she was now in shirt, pants and tooled leather boots, with her hair tied back, have been all set for a fast ride across some windswept plain.

Scrapes took the pipe from the grip of his few remaining teeth, narrowed his eyes and peered above him to the silhouetted shapes of the town rooftops and balconies, blind, blank windows and curl of soft smoke from the slumbering forge.

He swallowed. 'If you're about, Marshal, you're sure as hell goin' to have to make this quick. Time's runnin' out . . . ' He murmured the words to himself, his old eyes scanning steadily over the shapes against the flat night sky where the stars had come to life and the moon watched like an eye.

'What's that you're mutterin'?' asked Lately. 'What you sayin' there?'

'Nothin',' said Scrapes. 'Nothin' at all . . . '

* * *

A new deeper and more intense silence gripped the street as McConnell, the Judge and Charlton Folde were man-handled on to the crates and made to face the waiting townfolk.

'Take a good long look at these men,' boomed Lovell over the night air. His dark gaze began to gleam as if he could already see the dangling bodies. 'They're here as a warnin': any man here who gets to thinkin' himself smart enough to cross me, get in my way or figures he can — '

The bogus bounty hunters, Joe Doone and Ben Pullman fell in the first hail of rapid rifle fire that blazed from the darkness like a rush of searing flame.

The town crowd fell back, stunned and bewildered. Lovell's sidekicks sprang into life, at first jostling uselessly among themselves, some tripping and falling in the sudden panic to do something. Orders were shouted and ignored. Colorado Jack cracked a fist across a man's jaw as he threatened to fire a wild shot into the night sky.

'What you firin' at, you fool?' he yelled. 'Don't nobody shoot 'til we've got a target. Go find whoever did this.'

But too late for the sidekicks to make any purposeful move as another round of gunfire burst from the shadows, this time from the other side of the street to take out three men as they scrambled for cover.

'Find the sonofabitch!' screamed Lovell, grabbing Hedda Folde's arm and heading back to the bank. 'Clear the street and bring them prisoners back to me. Now, damnit!'

Scrapes lit his pipe in spite of the confusion around him. 'Marshal Brand,' he murmured. 'He made it. You bet he did!'

'You keep goin' on about him,' said Lately, trying to keep his balance against the fast disappearing town folk. 'You can't be certain.'

'Well, I got a gut feelin',' said Scrapes, releasing a cloud of smoke to the night. 'And when I get a gut feelin' — '

'You won't have nothin' if we don't shift,' snapped Doc. 'Get off the street. Find cover. There's somebody out here ain't finished yet!'

19

Seven bodies littered the far end of the street where the hanging tree stood thick and heavy, the noosed ropes still draped across the major bough, the crates kicked aside in the bloodstained dirt. Six of Lovell's men still breathing nursed wounds to hands, arms, legs; a seventh slumped in a dazed bewilderment of who and where he was, a pain throbbing mercilessly through his head.

Doc Munday moved quietly among them, treating where he could, bandaging where it was called for. Colorado Jack followed at his side.

'This is goin' to take time,' said Doc. 'I need more medicines, ointments, dressings . . . You'll have to get these men — those who can walk — to my surgery, top of the street.'

'We ain't got too much time, none at all for messin' with men who ain't goin' to be a deal of use,' said the gunslinger, spitting deep into the dust. 'Boss ain't for carryin' baggage. Specially after this.' He gestured to the street and black bulks of the deserted buildings. 'When we get our hands on the fella . . . '

'You mean Marshal Brand,' grinned Doc, his gaze tight on Colorado's face. 'I'm sure you've figured he did all this. It was his gun that opened up. And you never saw him and now I'll wager you won't find him.'

'Don't bank on it, Doc. I don't give a damn who the fella is, we'll find him if he's here. And when we do — '

'We goin' to do somethin' about these men?' asked Doc.

'Do what you can here, then we leave 'em. Them who can make it know the plan. They'll be there if they can walk.'

'That's about as callous as I've heard,' snapped Doc. 'I ain't no time for murderin' gunslingers, but hell, these men are human bein's. It ain't in my instinct — '

'When you ride with Jude Lovell, you know the rules,' quipped Colorado. 'Now do like I say, fast as you can. This street ain't safe.'

★ ★ ★

'Has he gone? He still here? What do you reckon, Jess?' Lately Poole rubbed his eyes, opened them wide, blinked and leaned back in the nest of straw bales in the livery barn. 'Hell, what's goin' to happen to Sheriff McConnell and the judge? And what about Folde, Milton Boyd and Hedda? Lovell goin' to kill 'em all?' He sighed. 'Mebbe he ain't done with the town yet. Mebbe he'll shoot it up like he threatened.'

Jess Morden grunted but held his gaze tight on what he could see of the street. 'Too many questions there for me, Lately. I ain't got a clue to what Brand's plannin' or where he is — if he's here at all. We ain't seen him. He ain't shown himself.'

His gaze moved slowly left to right,

left again, then settled on the bank. 'Right now I'm only interested in how many men Lovell's still got and what he's goin' to do next. He's got Doc busy down there cleanin' up. But what's comin'? Is he goin' to pull out with that wagon he's been loadin'?'

Lately struggled from the bales to join him. 'My bet would be that's exactly what he'll do. He came here for money and now he's got it he'll go. Hell, what's he got to stay for? He ain't goin' to risk givin' Marshal Brand another chance, is he? Would you?'

* * *

The long minute hand of the bank clock clunked to within a whisker of announcing midnight, faltered and ground through a mechanical belch.

'Time I did somethin' about that unreliable brute,' said Milton Boyd, consulting his own timepiece. 'Livin' on borrowed time, you might say,' he added with a shaky grin and quick, jerky glance across the bank's gloomy main floor to Sheriff McConnell, the judge, Hedda Folde and her husband.

The sheriff stiffened and went back to his concentration on Lovell, the sidekicks handling the sacks and boxes of money, and the attention being paid to every movement by the man they called the Dealer.

'We all through here?' asked Colorado Jack, keeping anxious watch at the open rear door. He eased aside to let another sidekick through with his cargo of cash to be added to the waiting wagon. 'Time we shifted before Brand gets busy again.'

'Brand?' snapped Lovell, looking up from the money-laden table. 'Who said anythin' about Brand? Who said he fired them shots?'

The Dealer's crimson jowls shook as he stacked another wad of notes between his podgy fingers. 'Who else?' he asked blandly. 'Do you know anybody else can handle a rifle like that? Winchester was always Marshal

Brand's speciality.' His jowls wobbled again. 'Colorado's right — it was Brand clear enough.'

'He don't bother me none,' huffed Lovell.

'Well, he should,' said the Dealer. 'He sure as hell bothers me! You should go take a look at the bodies out there.'

'I've seen 'em,' brooded Lovell, settling a dark glare on McConnell, Boyd and Hedda Folde. 'Time somebody paid.'

The Dealer stuffed the wad of notes into a bag and handed it to a sidekick.

'Forget it,' he said, taking his coat from the back of a chair. 'We've finished here. Let's move while we have the dark to help us. Time we put Saracen at our backs. Won't be a deal more than another day before word's spreadin' through the territory like plague about what's happened.' Purple veining patterned his chins. 'And this time there'll be genuine bounty hunters headin' our way in swarms!'

'He's right,' said Colorado, stepping aside again for a sidekick. 'Light won't be up for another three hours. That'll see us well clear of town and into the hills. Once there — '

'So who pays for them killed here?' growled Lovell. 'Matt Michaels, Ben, Joe Doone, Frank Mooney . . . they count for nothin'? They just rottin' for the worms?'

'Sound men, I'm sure,' said the Dealer, adjusting the set of his coat. 'But they're the dead, Jude. The past. If all the plannin' that's gone into this raid, all the time spent detailin' it out down to the last . . . if all that's goin' to mean anythin' at all, then now's the time to move. Matt, Ben, Joe, Frank, and any of the others lost to us, would agree.' He patted the coat into place. 'We take the woman there as hostage and pull out. Agreed?'

Lovell turned sharply to face McConnell, the judge, Folde and Boyd. 'You've stayed lucky,' he grinned covering a sneer. 'Real lucky. Mebbe I should've shot you first off, eh? Got rid of you.'

'Don't you go thinkin' you're goin' to get away with this,' began Boyd, his face flushing under a beading of sweat. 'I'll see you in — '

McConnell and the judge laid restraining hands on his arms.

Lovell spat fiercely across the floor, a hand dropping instinctively to the butt of his holstered Colt.

'Easy,' urged the judge.

'Leave it,' ordered the Dealer, his jowls gleaming with sweat. 'Don't waste time on them.'

Hedda Folde stepped forward, tossed her hair into her neck and stared defiantly into Lovell's eyes.

'All right, let's cut the talk and go, shall we?' She stood tall to her full height. 'I'm tired of guns and shootings, and the smell of money is getting on my nerves.'

Lovell's hand fell away from the Colt.

'Have no fear, Mrs Folde,' said the judge, 'we shall do everything in our power — '

'I'm sure,' clipped Hedda, her stare

still tight on Lovell's face. 'But like the Dealer here says, we're wasting time.'

Her husband's brow erupted in a fresh lathering of sweat that trickled slowly to the bridge of his nose, spread and headed left and right to his cheeks. 'Hedda, my dear, I just want you to know that anythin' you heard back there in the street — '

'I heard all I wanted to hear,' snapped Hedda. Her stare shifted sharply to his glazed gaze. 'As far as I'm concerned you can go to hell!' She swung back to Lovell. 'You ready to roll them wheels, mister?'

Lovell smiled. 'You got it, lady!'

The Dealer, Lovell and Hedda Folde headed for the door, the dark night beyond and the black bulk of the loaded wagon where the remaining sidekicks waited in the glow of a single lantern.

Colorado Jack urged them to quicken their pace. 'We've got horses all saddled and ready to go. Two fellas aboard the wagon. I'll ride point. We head direct to the hills, main trail at this hour, then into the Bigbones.'

'And then?' asked Hedda.

'Let's see if you make it that far, shall we?' grinned the gunslinger.

Jude Lovell was the last to leave the bank, turning slowly as he stepped into the night. He waited, unblinking, chillingly calm, then drew his Colt clear of leather and blazed two shots into Charlton Folde's gut.

'Like the lady said, go to hell!' he smiled.

20

They watched the dust clouds swirl on the night like a feeding frenzy of swarming midges. The noise of pounding hoofs, spinning wheels, creaking timbers and leather, jangling tack and shouted orders from dry throats clamoured across the air as if each would throttle the other. And within minutes Jude Lovell, his partners and sidekicks, his hostage, the wagon and its cargo of stolen money had cleared the main street and left Saracen stunned in a silence so thick it seemed there to be touched.

The bank clock had clunked on another half-hour before those watching from the bank, the groups of town folk gathered in the street, and Jess, Scrapes Tuppence and Lately Poole at the livery came out of their trance of bewilderment and chilled fear.

It was Milton Boyd who spoke first. 'So is that it?' he said, looking round the littered main office of the bank; the tossed aside books, boxes, files, the safe doors standing open, the empty shelves, bottles, stained glasses, stubbed-out cigars and smears of grey ash. He sniffed. 'Damn it, you can smell the rats! Place will never be the same.'

Judge Whinnie strode to the rear door and took in a deep breath of the night air. 'No,' he pronounced, his chest expanding, 'this is not it, as you put it, Mr Boyd. Far from it, I'd say. In fact, it would be my bettin' that Sheriff McConnell here is already shapin' up a plan in his mind. Am I right, Sheriff?'

'You bet,' bustled McConnell, tightening his gunbelt. 'Jude Lovell ain't going to make a laughin' stock of this town. Nossir. Saracen folk don't take kindly to that. So if he thinks he's ridden out of here with *our* money, stolen from *our* bank, leavin' us, he reckons, the miserable paupers, well, he can sure as hell figure again.'

He fixed a glinting stare on the judge's face. 'I'm goin' to round up them willin' to ride along of me and we're goin' to go right after that wagon. No waitin'. No messin'. And don't let any man forget that Lovell's taken Hedda Folde, and he'll kill her just whenever it suits. That ain't goin' to happen.' Sweat beaded on his brow. 'As for her husband there — '

'He got what was comin' to him,' snapped Boyd. 'But there's others who've died . . . ' His voice faltered, then rallied. 'I'm with you, Sheriff. All the way.'

Judge Whinnie cleared his throat and gazed thoughtfully into the darkness. 'I wonder where Marshal Brand's goin' to figure in all this?' he murmured softly to himself.

★ ★ ★

Precisely the same thought was turning in the mind of Doc Munday as he made his way to join Jess Morden at the livery.

Where was Brand? Was he still in town? He would have seen Lovell leaving, so had he followed? How would he get to tackling . . . But the questions had come too thick and fast for his mind to handle, and he had hurried on.

Jess was already busy preparing horses for the posse McConnell would be raising.

'I ain't heard it official yet,' said Jess, 'but there can't be any doubt we'll be ridin'. And it ain't just Lovell and the money we're thinkin' to. There's Hedda. And there ain't no way we're lettin' her die in Lovell's hands.'

'Say that again,' added Scrapes, giving Jess a helping hand. 'And I'll tell you somethin' else: we've got a whole heap of pride at stake here. Why, damnit, that sonofabitch gunslinger and his ratbag sidekicks have taken us and our town for nothin' less than mule-headed fools. We fell for his two-bit schemin', fell down the line, start to finish. And right now Lovell's gettin' away with it — or thinks he is.' The old man winked. 'We'll see, eh, Doc? He might not have the edge he's reckonin' on.'

'Well — ' began Doc, but was interrupted as Sheriff McConnell, Judge Whinnie and Lately Poole appeared through the shadowy gloom.

McConnell came bluntly to the point. 'We're ridin'. First hint of light. Anybody who figures he can help is welcome. More guns we have the better.' He turned to Lately. 'How do you fancy keepin' watch on the town while we're gone, Lately? The saloon, the store, what's left of the bank . . . this place if Jess is with us.'

'You bet to it,' said Jess.

Lately adjusted his hat and hitched his pants. 'Well, if you figure I can handle things here,' be began.

'Sure you can,' said McConnell. 'And you'll have Judge Whinnie alongside of you.'

He shifted his gaze again, this time to the wider sweep of the fast fading night sky. 'Another half-hour, then we ride,' he murmured. 'Lovell ain't goin' to make the progress he'll be reckonin' on, not with that wagon and the weight it's carryin'. He's goin' to have to give the team some rest up time.'

'Be all of a full day before he gets deep into the hills,' said Scrapes. 'I know, I've been in and out of the Bigbones with all manner of horses, wagons, you name it, for close on a lifetime. Lovell is goin' to find them rocks a deal unfriendly, unless you know 'em and can read 'em.'

'That's where we're goin' to need you, Scrapes,' said the sheriff. 'You were right there at the start of this,. Only fittin' you should be there at the end.'

The light began its struggle to break through the heavy night sky. There was a cooler, thinner edge to the air. But the sun would be there all too soon, thought Doc. And with it the heat.

The thoughts began to clamour again in his mind: the questions without answers; the jumbled images and sounds; gunshots, voices, creak and grind of wagon wheels.

'Best check out what we'll be needin',' said Jess quietly at his shoulder.

★ ★ ★

The mood in the town changed with the light. The hours of fear, doubt and the bleak prospect of Saracen being ravaged to the point of destruction, gave way to anger, resentment and an almost desperate need for retribution.

Folk gathered again in the street, this time free of the shadow of Lovell and his gunslingers, but deeply conscious of Hedda Folde being held hostage, awaiting a fate no one could predict; of the deaths of McConnell's deputies and Jim Squire, the travellers from the west and, though he had quickly lost his standing in the town, Charlton Folde. No one mourned or much cared about the loss of Lovell's men. They had earned their own agony.

'And then there's all that money,'

said a man, lighting a cheroot. 'Lord knows how much, but we've each and everyone of us got a stake in it. Damn it, it's Saracen money! Spent here, banked here. Big part of it would have gone towards all our futures. And that's why I'm joinin' up with the sheriff's posse. You bet I am! That money, and Mrs Folde, are comin' right back here — to Saracen!'

There had been cheered support for the man's resolve, but an old-timer had added caution.

'But don't go thinkin' it's goin' to be a picnic,' he warned. 'Lovell ain't goin' to give up that money without some hell of a fight. He spent a whole heap of time and effort plannin' the raid, and he knows, down to the last dollar, that he's got away with a fortune. Ask Milton Boyd. He'll sure as hell tell you! And Lovell's done it right under our very noses.' The old man had lifted his battered hat, scratched his bald head, rummaged in a waistcoat pocket for the butt end of a cigar, lit it and had blown thick grey smoke. 'He'll be spittin' like a liverish rattler. And it's goin' to take one very special man to tackle him.'

'Well,' said a lean man lounging casually in the shadows, 'mebbe Lovell's already met just such a fella. Could be he's still around, or leastways not far away. Could be we've all seen him, eh? Mebbe Marshal Brand's out there even now, followin' that wagon, just waitin' on the moment.'

★　★　★

Sheriff McConnell's posse of a dozen or so men pulled out as the light broke full enough for Lovell's tracks to be trailed with ease.

The loaded wagon had made steady progress on a part of the trail that offered few if any difficulties. Sand, loose rock, stragglings of rough brush had been no hindrance to the still fresh team as they and the outriders guarding the precious cargo took a direct route to the foothills.

'Any notions as to what Lovell's route's goin' to be?' McConnell had asked as he fell back to ride alongside Scrapes Tuppence.

'Way I'm figurin' it, he's got two choices,' said Scrapes. 'One: he could do the obvious and move deep into Chance Creek. Plenty of cover there and he could rest up without bein' seen for some time, if at all. But, like I say, it's obvious. It's simply stayin' with the main trail. Or two — and this would be my choice — he could make for Bearpaw Cut.'

'Hell, that's risky with a wagon and team, ain't it?' frowned McConnell.

'You bet it is. It's tougher goin', slower and takin' him a whole sight deeper. But, and here's the ace, it's safer if you're plannin' on stayin' out of sight. Hell, we could be trailin' through them rocks at the Cut for days and never catch a sight of the outfit, much less hear it. And remember, if it's tough for him, it's the same for us.'

McConnell rode in silence for a

while. 'So that's what you'd do, is it, Scrapes? You'd head for Bearpaw Cut and risk the goin'?'

'Wouldn't you, when you know for a dead certainty you're bein' followed? Lovell's got too much at stake now not to take a chance. After all, luck's been with him so far, ain't it?'

'Not all the way,' smiled the sheriff. 'There's been the little matter of Marshal Brand. And as far as I know, there still is.'

21

The sun was full up and fierce, the heat thickening, the flies pestering and the canteen water growing warmer by the hour when Scrapes and Sheriff McConnell brought the posse to a halt in the lee of a high rocky overhang.

'Rest up,' called the sheriff, wiping the sweat from his face with an already sodden bandanna. 'Ten minutes,' he added, spreading the bandanna to dry in the sun.

Doc Munday and Jess Morden slid gratefully from hot sticky saddles and tended the mouths of their mounts with welcomed wet rags.

Milton Boyd remained mounted, his fingers flicking anxiously, repetitively through the slowly furling pages of a notebook, his eyes in turn narrowing then widening, in one moment black and narrowed, in the next round, glassy and increasingly bloodshot.

'Hell,' he said at last, 'it's worse than I thought. Worse than that, it's a disaster. There can't have been nothin' like it in the history of this territory's bankin'. If not national bankin'. World bankin'.' Sweat dripped freely from his chin to the pages. 'Hell,' was all he could murmur.

'I won't ask how much,' said Doc. 'Wouldn't seem to be decent.'

'And you'd be right,' agreed Boyd, continuing to flick through the pages, front to back, back to front and back again. 'If I'm anywhere near right — and I ain't noted for slack figurin' — Lovell's packed that wagon with enough money to —

'Ain't no point in wastin' your breath on it,' clipped McConnell sharply. 'Fact is, however much he's taken, he's holdin' it and you ain't.' His gaze darkened. 'He's also got Mrs Folde.'

Boyd snapped the notebook shut. 'I wasn't suggestin' — '

'Nobody said you were,' interrupted

Jess. 'It's just a question of seein' things as they are. A wagonload of money — a hundred wagons — don't buy a human life.'

Scrapes Tuppence cleared his throat for attention. 'Speakin' of things as they are, our situation right now ain't good.'

'How come?' asked one of the riders.

'Bearpaw Cut's comin' up,' continued Scrapes, 'and I'm certain Lovell's taken that route. But right now, all's quiet — a touch too quiet by my reckonin' — and there ain't been the slightest sight of that wagon. Now — '

'Hold it,' hissed Jess suddenly, a hand shielding his eyes as his gaze tightened on the scrawl of the shimmering rock slopes and starker peaks. 'Somebody's up there. Watchin' us. How long's he been there?'

* * *

Doc Munday, Sheriff McConnell, Scrapes and the others of the posse joined Jess in his tight gaze on the tumbled rocks, following the line of his raised arm to pinpoint the spot.

'Up there. Right there,' he said quietly.

'Where?' asked a man, his eyes already streaming with sweat. 'Where f'Chris'sake?'

'There,' urged Jess. 'Movin'. Right now.'

Eyes narrowed. No one spoke. Sweat trickled. Horses snorted and tossed heads against pestering flies.

'Got it!' grunted a man with a floppy brimmed hat pushed to the back of his head. 'I see him. Top of that beaky crag. Touch to the right.'

Heads moved as one. Hands closed to shade eyes. Breathing wheezed against the heat. Trickles of sweat deepened.

'He's movin'.'

'More to the right.'

'Waitin' now.'

'Could be he's tryin' to show us somethin'.'

Doc took a step forward. 'Mebbe he is at that,' he murmured. 'Could be it's a sign . . . like he's pointin' somethin' out.'

'Ain't nothin' worth the showin' up there,' grunted Scrapes. 'Just a whole heap of scorchin' rocks and rattlers' nests. I been up there many a time. Why, I can recall — '

'He ain't *showin'* us nothin',' said Jess. 'He's *tellin'* us. Tellin' us which way to go.'

'Damnit, you're right,' said McConnell. 'We're too far east. Lovell's outfit's turned to the north.'

'But how in hell does *he* know — the fella up there?' asked the man with the floppy hat, peering from under it as the brim fell forward. 'Who in God's name is he?'

'Could only be one man, couldn't it?' muttered Jess, shielding his eyes again. 'It's gotta be Brand.'

★　★　★

Was it Brand? Could it be that the marshal had trailed Lovell and the wagon through the night? Only that way, surely, could he pinpoint the outfit's progress. It *had* to be Brand — leastways, that was the prospect McConnell wanted to believe and his posse needed as the impetus to take them on through the increasing heat and worsening terrain.

'If he's movin' directly north,' mused Scrapes, between flourishes of his bandanna across his glistening face, 'he's takin' on the worst of the Cut. Would have been a whole sight easier to drag that outfit closer to the east.'

'So what's his thinkin'?' wondered Jess.

The men mounted up in silence.

'Lovell knows we'll be followin',' said one of the town men as the posse moved off. 'He's mebbe got look-outs posted even now, keeping a watch on us. So mebbe he's figurin' on makin' life as tough as possible for us. Worse it gets, more likely we are to give up.'

'And he ain't no fool, is he?' added the man riding alongside him. 'He knows we ain't goin' to rush an attack while ever he's holdin' Mrs Folde.'

'Or mebbe he's figurin' another way,' said Doc, as the line of riders picked their slow way through the rocks under a cloudless sky and searing sun. 'Suppose he plans to ditch the wagon. Unload it when he's good and ready, distribute the money among the men, then scatter. We'd be hard pushed then to keep up the chase.'

Boyd grunted. 'Makes some sense, but shiftin' that amount of money in these conditions . . . Hell, it's all a fella can do to keep himself and his horse upright, let alone ride with a weight of cash slung round him.'

'He could be plannin' on hidin' it,' offered Jess. 'That wouldn't be difficult up here. He could bury the cash — mebbe in a cave or creek — clear the mountains and come back later. We ain't goin' to be prowlin' these mountains forever, are we?'

'You're right about the caves and creeks,' said Scrapes. 'Any number up here, and you could ride right by some a dozen times and never see 'em. Oh, yes, if it's a hidin' place you're lookin' for . . . '

It was the slow rumbling roar of land on the move that drowned Scrapes's words; a roar that deepened, rolled, shuddered, seemed to hang, then rushed on like the beat of stampeding cattle.

'Landslide!' yelled Jess.

'Take cover!' echoed McConnell.

A dust cloud blotted out the glare of the sun. Horses snorted, whinnied, bucked. Riders wrestled reins to keep control. The line of the posse broke as men steered their mounts to wherever there seemed the hope of shelter against the oncoming but still unseen slide.

'That ain't no natural happenin',' coughed Scrapes against the swirling dust.

'What you sayin'?' wheezed McConnell, blinking dirt from his eyes as more settled like frost on his sweat-stained stubble.

'Somebody started this. Up there. On them slopes.' He pointed blindly into the dust cloud.

'Lovell?' wheezed McConnell again.

'Gotta be. Only scum like him would . . .'

Scrapes's words were lost for the second time as an explosion ripped into the gathering momentum of tumbling rocks, throwing dirt, stone, earth high into the air. It showered down again like black rain.

'F'Chris'sake, that's dynamite!' bellowed Jess, his voice cracking as he choked on the dust. 'Lovell's blowin' the mountain apart!'

★ ★ ★

It certainly felt that way to Doc. The roar of cascading rocks and rubble, the boom of the explosion, the sounds of frightened horses, shouts and croaking voices, and the spinning echoes spiralling through the caverns, creeks and gulches to the highest peaks, rang in his ears until he thought they would burst.

Doc stumbled, reeled, held on for dear life to the reins as his mount bucked and threatened a wild-eyed dash into oblivion. Other riders around him did their best to stay upright themselves and calm the near panic-stricken horses.

McConnell was almost on his knees, his shouts and curses lost in the confusion and echoing noise. Scrapes Tuppence and Jess Morden struggled in a dust-swirling mêlée of horses, thrashing hoofs, bodies, arms and legs. Milton Boyd had already crashed to the ground and lost his mount.

It was only minutes but seemed like a nightmarish hour before the horses settled, the dust began to clear and McConnell's men blinked on the havoc around them.

'Steady the horses there!' he called, urging the riders to forget their own pains and concentrate on the valuable mounts. A fellow out here without a horse was a man facing the agony of a lingering death.

Doc cleared his eyes, his ears, his head and turned his attention to the men nursing cuts, grazes, pulled muscles and bruising from the flying rocks and stones.

The vague track they had been following was no more. 'Gone,' was Scrapes's blunt pronouncement, as he scratched his head and tried to fathom a new way to the north. 'Lovell was on to us and he sure as hell was all for stoppin' us.'

'Made a darn good job of it too,' wheezed a man, brushing the dust from his hat and shirt. 'What do we do now? Turn back, find another way, wait for that fella up there to do somethin'?'

'Brand can't face Lovell and his men alone,' said Doc, applying a rough bandage to a man's arm. 'There's got to be a way we can somehow — '

A shattering hail of gunfire ripped into the rocks and dirt like the breaking of a violent mountain storm.

22

Men ducked, dived, stumbled and scrambled like bemused ants for whatever cover was nearest. Some made it to larger boulders; some fell flat on their stomachs behind the meanest of rocks left in the wake of the landslide.

McConnell barked orders as he flattened himself against a rock face and peered for a sight of where the gunmen were positioned. 'Stay low,' he shouted. 'No firin' back 'til we've got targets.'

'Main shootin's to our left,' called Jess. 'Top of that slope.'

Heads craned to pinpoint the spot. More shots rang out, whined and echoed across the gulches, creeks and rifts to the peaks. Horses snorted and pawed. The sun blazed. Men sweated.

'I got two badly wounded back here,' said Doc, doing the best he could to staunch the flow of blood from a man's arm.

'Another here,' shouted a man.

'Lenny Farr's dead,' groaned a youth, his eyes blazing with a mixture of fear and anger. 'You hear? Lenny's — '

'We hear you,' snapped McConnell. 'Just don't get to joinin' him. Keep your head down, f'Chris'sake!'

Milton Boyd felt his body would melt in the heat and confusion. He glanced to left and right, hopeful that he might find a deeper, safer cover than the already bullet-chipped and scarred boulder sheltering him. There was nothing. The caves were too high, the shadowy creeks too distant. He was a prisoner where he lay. A body slipping back to liquid.

'Listen up,' called McConnell, between bursts of gunfire. 'Them guns of Lovell's are too high. Me and Jess will see if we can get closer. Mebbe give that marshal a hand if he's still breathin'. The rest of you stay where you are. Cover Jess and me when we make our move. You got that? Round up them horses best you can, then stay hidden. Jess — you fit to move?'

'Right along of you, Sheriff,' he answered.

'Good, then let's go.'

* * *

They squirmed away, McConnell leading as he made for a deeper, thicker wall of rocks thrown up in the blast. Three fast rounds of gunfire from the men behind them drew the concentration of Lovell's sharp-shooters just long enough for Jess and the sheriff to make it to the cover and wait, panting like hounds, sweat dripping freely from their chins.

'There's an outcrop to the right there that looks promisin',' said Jess, wiping his face. 'More cover and a clearer view of the range beyond the slope. If Brand's still with us, I'd wager for him bein' somewhere there.'

'You could be right at that,' murmured McConnell, narrowing his eyes on the shimmer and glare ahead. 'I hadn't reckoned for Lovell standin' to fight so soon. Thought he'd keep that wagon movin', lure us on deeper.'

'Mebbe he rates his chances while his men are still fresh. If he could break our backs here, he's got a clear run north. Wouldn't be a soul stoppin' him.'

'Yeah, well, that ain't goin' to happen. We're stickin' right with him. You agree?'

'Tight as leeches,' grinned Jess. He glanced quickly to his right. 'Let's make it to that boulder.'

They shifted again, this time without the threat of Lovell's gunfire, and made it to the boulder in a slither of arms and legs.

'Now what?' hissed McConnell.

Jess scanned the slope, its lifts and falls, craggy lines, scattered rocks and bleak, remorseless barrenness. His thoughts tumbled through a clutter of images. He was back again in the crowded town street on the day Lovell was brought in by the bounty hunters. He could hear the calls, the jeers, the mocking anger of a crowd drawing its bravado from the sight of the gunslinger roped to his mount, eyes downcast, shoulders slumped. Some men had spat, some thrown trash and handfuls of dirt. All had joined in the heady expectation of the hanging that would surely follow, as certain as day to night.

But how soon the mood had changed on Lovell's escape. How quickly the panic, sheer fear and dread had set in as Lovell and his positioned men had taken control. Then the shadow of death had shifted to those who had spat and jeered — and they had fled faster than flies from a downpour.

And where were those same men now, damn it? Not here in these rocks, this dust and dirt and godforsaken heat. Lovell must be laughing till the tears were streaming . . .

'Somethin's happenin',' hissed McConnell. 'Lovell's men are movin'. I can see them, hear them. Goddamn it, they must've seen us.'

Guns blazed from the men of the posse, but drew no response from Lovell's men. Another burst of fire, another . . . and still no answering shots.

'Unless I'm very much mistaken Lovell's men are circling to the back of our boys.' Jess screwed his eyes tight against the glare and peered harder. 'Hell, they'll be pickin 'em off like rats in a barrel unless we — '

A splintering crash of timbers, spin and grind of wheels, thrash of leather and suddenly clouding dust, filled the air and silenced the guns.

'What in the name of tarnation — ?' spluttered McConnell, erupting in a new surge of sweat.

'It's Hedda, f'Chris'sake,' yelled Jess. 'She's taken over the wagon. But how come? How'd she manage — '

'Where's Lovell?'

'She ain't never goin' to handle that,' shouted Jess, against the thundering crashes of the wagon as it bounced and slithered over rocks and through the strips and slivers of sand and dirt. 'There ain't no track.' He squirmed like a snake in the cover. 'She needs help, damnit!'

Jess was on his feet and staggering towards the wagon in seconds.

'For God's sake, Jess, you'll get yourself killed,' yelled McConnell, coming to his knees and then jerkily upright.

A single shot spat rock at his side. A second whined at Jess's heels. A third shot; four — and soon a hail peppering McConnell's position and zinging after Jess like a nest of demented hornets.

McConnell sank back into cover and narrowed his gaze on the men of the posse and the still circling figures of the gunslingers. No sign of Lovell. So how had Hedda managed to wrench herself and the wagon free of whoever had been guarding her and the bank haul? What of the Dealer and Colorado Jack?

He shook his head against the confusion of thoughts, cleared the sweat from his face and swung round again at a thicker, deeper crash and ear-splitting scream of spinning wheels on hot axles.

Hedda had been unable to hold the racing team against a headlong dash for a sprawl of larger boulders. They had smashed into the first, snorted, sweated, but raced on. It was the second — a razor-edged brute of a mound — that had been too much for the already straining wheels. The wagon had crashed full on to the boulder's thickest side and slewed crazily to the right, then the left, back to a level course again, only to slew a second time and threaten to topple on its side.

Hedda fought madly with the reins, at first trying to slow the team and bring them to a halt, but at a shout from Jess to let the horses run she slackened her grip.

The wagon bounced, creaked, groaned as Hedda wrestled now to settle the outfit back on its wheels. A shattering, deepening groan warned of worse to come as the horses, blind now in their panic, heaved the wagon ever closer to a shelving slope to the left.

Jess staggered on, desperate to come closer to the wagon, conscious of what he could already see was going to happen once the horses broke free and the wagon continued under its own momentum.

'Jump! Get clear!' he yelled, through the choking swirls of dust and flying dirt.

Hedda appeared not to hear him in the shattering mix of noise to which the horses had now added their echoing whinnies of panic.

'Jump!' yelled Jess again, almost falling flat as he lost his footing and fought to keep his balance.

He risked a hurried glance back. No sight of McConnell; nothing either of Lovell, the town posse or the gunslingers. But the firing, spasmodic now and more a threat than with targets in mind, still whined and echoed through the rocky chasms, drifts and shimmering peaks.

He swung his gaze hack to the outfit.

The wagon bounced as if receiving a knockout punch. He wiped sweat from his face as Hedda began to fall under the swish and sway of the weight beneath her.

'Jump, f'Chris'sake.'

This time she jumped, or more likely was thrown. She seemed for a moment to sail across the glaring light in a twisting shimmer of arms, legs and body, was lost in the dust cloud, then there again, thudding to the ground as lifeless as any of the rocks around her.

Jess cursed and scrambled on disregarding now the sight of the horses free of the wagon, the scattered splinters of timber, entrails of broken reins and tack, and headed directly for the woman.

He paused only briefly at the point where the wagon had slid across the slope to the rocks and creek below. It had rolled crazily, spewing its cargo of boxed and bagged bank money high and wide, and finally crashed to matchwood and still spinning wheels in what might have been its graveyard.

23

Sheriff McConnell watched the sky fill with floating money. Dollar bills drifted as if in a carefree flock high above the creek bed where the wagon had come to shattered grief. Some notes soared, caught in an uplift of air, others hovered like birds desperate to come to roost, and some spun into cracks and clefts among the rocks, or were impaled on the spiky tongues of rough brush and skeletal sage, there to flap against the faintest breeze until torn apart.

The gunfire had ceased and a thick, eerie silence settled in the mountain range. Dust clouds thrown up in the dash of the runaway wagon drifted like slow shrouds. McConnell could see nothing of Jess or Hedda Folde, and nothing for a while of Lovell's men or those of his own posse. What in the name of sanity had happened here in what seemed now little more than the blinking of an eye? What had happened to Jess and Hedda? What, damn it, of Lovell, and how would his men react now?

He had some of his answers in an instant.

The sight of the drifting money and the prospect of the scattered mass of coins and gold in the creek had been too much for the Dealer to stomach, and without a care for his skin and disregarding the posse's guns, he had risen out of cover to slither, slide, scramble any way he could to the waiting prize in the creek.

The sight of him, his grasping hands as he moved among the dollar bills, his eyes bloodshot with effort in his sweating face, his bulk moving through the dirt like a frantic slug, had been too much for the rest of Lovell's men. They broke their cover as one and with no more than a burst of wild fire as a token defiance, headed for the creek.

'Let 'em go,' ordered McConnell, as he too broke cover and joined the town men. 'Minute they're all down there in that creek, you pin 'em tight and don't let none of the rats out 'til we're good and ready. Meantime — '

'Jess and Mrs Folde,' prompted Doc anxiously.

'Take Scrapes here and go find 'em,' said McConnell. 'I just hope . . . Yeah, well, let's just hope, eh?'

'What about the money?' blustered Boyd from the sodden depths of a gushing sweat. 'We can't just leave it like that in the dirt. It ain't right. Damnit, it don't belong in dirt.'

'Gather what you can, but don't take risks,' ordered McConnell. 'The money ain't a priority; Lovell is.' He shielded his eyes against the shimmers and glare. 'Now just what in hell is he doin'?'

'And where is he?' added Scrapes. 'And who's with him? I don't see nothin' of Colorado Jack.'

★   ★   ★

Jess waited for the flicker; for the eyelids that would open suddenly and show him that Hedda Folde was conscious and had survived the ordeal of driving the wagon until it had finally crashed and she had jumped clear.

He tried again to cushion her head on his thigh, dab tentatively at the cuts on her forehead with his bandanna and shield her as best he could in the rock outcrop from the merciless glare of the high sun.

He squinted to take in the surroundings. They were some distance from the slope, McConnell's men and what remained of Lovell's gang. He had seen the money scatter and watched the frantic dash to gather what could be found of the haul. But it was Lovell who worried him and still lifted a tingle of chill in the back of his neck.

His attention came sharply back to the woman as she stirred and opened her eyes.

'Lovell . . . he's making a run for it,' she murmured, stifling a wince. 'Him and Colorado. They've got horses. They've taken money, much as they can carry. Heading back the way they came.'

'Back towards town?' frowned Jess.

Hedda nodded, winced again and shifted her legs.

'How did you manage to grab the wagon like that?'

A faint grin flickered across Hedda's lips. 'There was just Lovell, Colorado Jack and one sidekick along of the wagon, plus myself, o'course, though I doubt if I rated a deal. Nobody was taking much notice of me — which suited me fine for what I had in mind.'

Hedda eased her bruised and aching legs to a more comfortable position and cleared the sweat from her face. 'You know what — Lovell knifed the sidekick clean between the shoulders. Killed him outright just where he stood, never a murmur.'

'Why?' gulped Jess.

'Clear as a creek stream from where I was watching: him and Colorado planned to move out, the pair of them with as much of the haul as they could carry. Then they got to stashing some in the rocks to collect later.' Hedda paused and swallowed. 'That's when I got busy. All Lovell and Colorado could see and do, involved counting, packing, hiding money, so I just grabbed the reins, slapped the team into action and trusted to luck and the Almighty! God knows where I thought I was going or for how long I could keep it up. But it seems like it worked — leastways for now.' She winced, closed her eyes and took a deeper breath.

'You bet it worked,' smiled Jess. 'There's money scattered like it was snow and Lovell's men scrambling after it frantic as flies.' He waited for Hedda to open her eyes. 'Did you see anythin' of the marshal?'

'Saw him soon after Lovell set up that landslide. He's up there somewhere. Trouble is, Lovell knows he is. And there's sure as hell room for only one of them . . . '

Sheriff McConnell knew he was being watched, even before he heard the slow trickle of disturbed pebbles, and fall of a boot to rock.

He froze where he stood wedged between boulders in his attempt to climb to the spot where Brand had last been seen. His hands flattened on the baking rocks. His eyes stung. His throat was dry, his thoughts already reeling back and forth in a swish of blurred images.

'That you, Marshal?' he croaked, his eyes closing on the hope.

'You got it,' said the voice at his back. 'Ease around, real slow, but stay low. Lovell ain't far away.'

McConnell did as he was told to finally face the dark, weathered face of Marshal Brand. 'Heck, am I glad to see you,' he rasped through a hissed murmur. 'We thought you might have pulled clear. Then we saw you. Hell, if this ain't some caper and a half!'

Brand grinned quickly and grunted, his eyes sharp as a hawk's on the surrounding rocks. 'Mrs Folde's been busy,' he said at last. 'Lovell's men and the Dealer are scavengin' down there like crows.'

'My men are coverin' the creek,' said McConnell. 'They can snaffle as much money as they like, they ain't goin' no place with it.' He paused a moment. 'What the hell is Lovell's game?'

'He's mebbe figured there's a whole lot too many guns gettin' too close. Looks to me like him and Colorado have decided to pull out with what they can carry. Should've figured that back there at the bank.' Brand wiped a trickle of sweat from his chin. 'That was always Lovell's weakness: he gets to plannin' a big haul, only to have his greed weigh him down. Like a fella with a big belch that keeps him at the table!' Brand's gaze narrowed. 'But right now he's fit enough and still deadly enough.'

McConnell ran a knuckle into his tired eyes. 'Seems to me these past days have been like a nightmare. When I think back to them bounty hunters trailin' Lovell into my town like he was — '

The single shot blazed, whined, echoed high as if to clip the topmost peak, and McConnell fell back, blood pouring from a wound in his shoulder.

★ ★ ★

Brand's reaction was instinctive. He had pushed McConnell deeper into the rocks even before the second shot had raged.

'Stay there!' he ordered. 'Don't move. Do the best you can with that wound.'

'Hell!' hissed the sheriff, gritting his teeth as he fumbled to staunch the blood flow with his bandanna. 'Is that . . . that Lovell up there?'

'Him and Colorado. More likely Colorado. Lovell would've blown your head off.'

'We've gotta move,' said McConnell.

'If we're in their sights . . . '

'You stay where you are. You ain't goin' to be of use with that wound.'

McConnell grimaced. 'Thanks — that makes me feel a whole sight better! And you, I suppose — '

But by then Marshal Brand had slid away.

24

Brand stifled a groan and took a deep breath before finding the strength from somewhere to climb on. He was way too old for this, he decided; too old, too tired and, if he were honest, past it. His days of upholding the law and bringing to book the likes of Jude Lovell and his miserable sidekicks were over. Even so, there were no two-bit gunslingers breathing who were going to come between him and that cabin on the river. No chance.

One last effort . . .

He reached a new nest of boulders, paused and looked back. McConnell had seen good sense and buried himself still deeper in the rocks. His men had slid into cover above the creek where the Dealer and a handful of men were still scrambling among the scattered money, some now so heavy and bloated with the haul stuffed into shirts and pockets that they could only waddle.

Brand half smiled to himself, but narrowed his eyes in tight concentration on the rocks ahead and around him. Colorado Jack's shot had been designed to lure the marshal out of cover. It had worked. But had Colorado been able to track Brand since he had left the sheriff? Maybe he had lost him. Maybe he was leaving him to Lovell.

He grunted quietly, found a new foothold and moved on with fast, rapid steps that worked up another lathering of sweat and the aching pains in his joints. Damn Jude Lovell. Damn the fake bounty hunters! Damn Saracen! And damn the bad luck that had brought him across those bluegrass plains.

His breath caught in his throat at the glimpse he had of Colorado almost directly ahead of him, his body half turned as if in concentration of something or someone below him. Close enough for a shot? Brand's fingers tapped the butt of his Colt. If he missed, if Colorado ducked away . . . Was Lovell with him?

The marshal eased a step forward. He risked another. A third. Something was wrong. He could sense it, almost smell it. Thirty years of tracking gunslingers, knowing the ways they thought and moved had taught him a harsh lesson: gunmen survived on their wits and an uncanny animal instinct. But this one was different. This one was so still he might have been dead. Or was it a new tactic?

Brand watched carefully. What had Colorado seen that he found so intriguing, almost to the point of being transfixed by it? His gaze narrowed. He licked his lips, drew his Colt, then lowered himself to feel for a loose stone at his feet. He found it, tightened his fingers around it and tossed it to within a couple of feet of Colorado's left boot.

The stone clattered and came to rest. Nothing happened. Colorado did not move. Brand slid his tongue over a trickle of sweat, and frowned. So still he might have been dead, he thought again.

Damnit, he was dead!

Brand tensed instantly, his body turning for whatever might be at his back, then to his right. He had walked into a trap, a dead man offered as bait. Had Lovell killed him? Did that mean — ?

The mocking laughter seemed to cascade from above him like a rush of released water. He looked up, his eyes straining against the glare, his bulk falling flat to the harshness of a pitted boulder.

'That's right, Marshal, he's dead,' cracked Lovell from somewhere in the maze and clutter of rocks. 'That's Colorado. Served his purpose, ain't he? Got his due shares, you might say!'

The laughter spilled again, almost manic in its cackle. Lovell could see him, but he could not see Lovell. Brand could only guess at where in the clutter he might be.

'I'd go easy there, if I were you,' called Lovell. 'I've got you covered, Marshal. There ain't much in the way of any place to go, so I'd pull out real fast, while you're still breathin'. You hear me down there?'

Brand stayed silent, planning now where he might move and when. Lovell's patience would not be at its most generous right now. He licked his lips, steadied his grip on the Colt and glanced quickly to where he had left the sheriff. All quiet. Either McConnell was doing exactly as ordered, or had passed out. Or had he moved?

'You movin', Marshal?' Lovell's voice had a keener edge. 'You're gettin' this chance only once. I ain't for delayin' none. I've got urgent matters need lookin' to.'

Brand waited a moment. 'You're wastin' your time, Lovell,' he shouted, levelling his tone against a deepening dryness in his throat. 'It's all over. You've lost the money and you're on your own. And there's others headin' this way right now. Dozens of 'em. So where you goin' to run to? You can't live in these mountains. Money ain't worth a snitch up here.'

Every word uttered had seen Brand slide another foot along the surface of the boulder. Lovell had offered no threat — so far. But not for long, he reckoned.

Lovell's gun blazed, the shot whining as it skimmed across the boulder. Brand ducked, quickened his movements and reached a deeper, darker cleft in the rocks. Wide enough for a body? He squeezed into it. But where did it lead? Had he walked into another trap?

Hell! He winced as he pushed his body into the cleft, then waited, sweat pouring down his face, and listened. Nothing. Silence. Even the men in the creek scrambling for money had fallen quiet. But where was Lovell now? Had he backed off or was he climbing down to finish the job at point-blank range?

He took stock of where he was. The cleft tunnelled like a chimney for some twelve, perhaps fifteen feet. He could see the clear light where it emerged as an opening on to what might be a plateau. Was that where Lovell was waiting? Did he know Brand was in the cleft?

There was only one way to find out.

He holstered his Colt, pressed his body tight to the rock at his back and began to ease himself upwards, painful inches at a time. The rock scraped the skin from his back; sweat flowed and dripped like water from a leaking pail. He wanted to moan out loud to relieve the ache in every muscle of his straining legs. But one sound and he was a sitting target.

It was some minutes before the marshal was able to pause within a foot or so of the opening. Now for the reality, the bitter truth of his effort. He clenched his teeth, took a deep breath and braced himself for the push.

He broke from the cleft like a gopher reaching light, blinked on the suddenness of the glare and searing heat and looked around him. He had been right; he had reached a small plateau, but there was neither sight nor sound of Lovell. He cursed and crawled to the far side overlooking what he guessed would be the spot where Hedda Folde had crashed the wagon. Sure enough, there were the scattered veins of reins and tack, some slivers of timber and here and there, pinned to the sage and brush like forlorn blooms, bank notes from the haul.

And there too was Lovell, with Hedda tight in his grip and Jess Morden sprawled at his feet.

★   ★   ★

Lovell began to laugh. 'Ain't you havin' a merry dance, Marshal?' he quipped, jabbing the barrel of his gun into Hedda's ribs. 'Thought you were never goin' to make it there. Came the long way, eh?' His grin spread to a mocking smile. 'Well, like you can see, I'm sorry to say all that effort was wasted. Such a pity! Bet you figured you had a real edge there for a minute,' he laughed. 'Got to see the funny side, ain't you? I mean, all that chasin' about and them shootin's and bodies and, Lord knows what, and look at us — I still win, don't I?'

Hedda tried to twist against Lovell's hold, but only succeeded in raising the pain in her shoulder wound.

'Still let's cut all the chasin' and talkin', shall we, and get to the serious business of me ridin' out of here?' Lovell steadied his stance and tightened his grip on his Colt. 'Now I got me two horses hitched back there in the rocks. One's packed with all the money I'm ever goin' to need, and the other's for carryin' me and the lady on our trek out of these mountains to the border. Clear enough so far?'

Brand merely watched in silence from his place on the plateau.

'Good,' continued Lovell. 'You're beginnin' to understand me, I see. That's right on the button, mister, just as I like it. 'Course, it goes without sayin', don't it, that any attempt — *any* attempt — by you or the scumbags hereabouts to stop me and . . . You're right, fella, the lady here gets it. Painful as I can make it. Understood? Do we have a deal? I leave; you leave; no more killin'; no more chasin'; and we all live happily ever after, as they say. The livery owner here gets to live and so does the sheriff and your good self. I like that. Neat and tidy, eh? No loose ends, 'ceptin' o'course, for the little matter of a hangin' that never happened. Guess that was a real *loose end*, eh, if you get my meanin'! But, as I always say — '

'You louse! You filthy, sonofa-goddamn-bitch rat! Why, I oughta hang you myself, and would, too, after all the two-faced double dealin' . . . '

The Dealer's voice and the torrent of words that bubbled from his mouth as if at boiling point, forced Lovell to break his hold on Hedda, push her aside and blaze a torrent of gunfire into the lumbering man as he stumbled through the rocks from the creek.

Brand seized his moment. He launched himself at full speed from the plateau, flying feet first through the air like some giant hawk swooping for the kill. He heard the roar of Lovell's gun, Hedda Folde's anguished scream, the sudden whinnying of horses; felt the rush of air across his face sending the sweat high in a glittering spray, then the tremor through his legs as he thudded to the ground.

He had his Colt clear of its holster in an instant. Lovell swung round from his destruction of the Dealer, a smile folding and creasing across his lips for a snarl, his eyes fierce with anger and the darkening reality of having lost the edge.

Brand lunged on, gun blazing, the momentum of his leap and the charge across the rocks gathered in a single burst of speed and resolve. He saw Lovell's gun slip from his fingers, saw the blood staining his shirt, spreading like night, and then the final moment

when the man's eyes rolled to the hills
and peaks, the cloudless sky and searing
sun and Jude Lovell was no more.

A lone hawk screeched and silence
closed in.

25

There was a fresher, keener edge to the air when the line of riders cleared the last of the Bigbones foothills and trailed at a gentle pace into the bluegrass plains. They had been moving since first light, anxious now to deliver their grisly burden of bodies to Saracen's Boot Hill and finally to rest their weary mounts and their own aching bodies.

The line was led by Sheriff McConnell, his shoulder heavily strapped, Marshal Brand and Doc Munday, with Hedda Folde and Jess Morden riding along of him. McConnell's posse of town men, closely shepherded along the trail by Scrapes Tuppence, brought up the rear line of bodies roped to spare mounts, three pack horses under the watchful gaze of Milton Boyd, and two men riding guard.

'So what's the final count then?'

asked Doc, easing his fingers through the reins. 'Two wounded, Mrs Folde here near exhausted, half-a-dozen dead bodies, includin' Lovell, Colorado Jack and the Dealer, and what could be saved of the bank haul. I missed anythin'?'

'Mebbe three of Lovell's men got clear,' said Scrapes, relaxing his freshly lit corncob pipe between his teeth. 'Stuffed their pockets and shirts full of money and bolted fast as they could for the high peaks.'

'Don't give a deal for their chances up there without food and water,' murmured Jess. 'And they ain't got horses — and ain't likely to find any neither.'

'Well, by my reckonin' we came out of all this a whole sight better than looked likely at one time,' added Doc. 'And that's thanks mainly to the marshal here.'

The riders nodded and grunted their agreement, most of them too tired, too weary from the demanding terrain and unremitting heat to recall the last minutes of Jude Lovell's life. It was enough that the man was dead.

'You'll be turnin' in the badge from here on,' said McConnell, glancing quickly at Brand. 'You got plans?'

'Long-standin' plans,' grinned the marshal. 'Thought I'd never get to 'em. And yourself — you stickin' with Saracen?'

'It's my town,' reflected McConnell, easing the binding on his shoulder. 'Helped build it. Ain't for leavin' it now. And 'sides, sad to say, there's always goin' to be another Jude Lovell ridin' in from somewhere. Some fast-gun young 'un who fancies his chance. Goes with the territory — and the badge, which I'm still wearin', thanks to you. Doubt if — '

'Forget it,' said Brand. 'Like you say, comes with the job.'

They rode on in silence, the far horizon and the prospect of Saracen soothing their thoughts as the full light broke.

* ★ ★

'You wouldn't have believed it. Nossir, not ever.' Scrapes Tuppence acknowledged the arrival of a clean glass and fresh bottle of whiskey at his corner table and surveyed his audience with an almost regal satisfaction.

He poured himself a generous measure, raised the glass to his benefactor and sank the drink in a single gulp. He smacked his lips and smiled as his enthralled audience waited.

'We came in from the bluegrass that day expectin' to find Saracen much as we'd left it. But, hell, no! Were we in for some surprise. The town was packed; main street here, full, saloon crowded and booming — all them folk who'd pulled out sick with the fear of Lovell and the retribution he would reap, were back, right there like they'd never left. Soon as they'd gotten to hear Lovell had pulled out with the money, they returned. And, boy, oh, boy, did we have some party.

"'Course, all that was a year back now, and things have simmered down again. Sheriff McConnell's got himself a smart new office; Lately Poole is runnin' the store along of his barberin' business; Jess Morden's livery is always busy now that we're on the stage route, and even Milton Boyd at the bank is a happy man again, countin' out the new money passin' his way. And, o'course, here at the Garter Saloon, Mrs Folde is a gem of her own kind. None finer. Keeps a decent whiskey too.'

An eager, middle-aged man in a tailored suit and sporting a grey derby leaned forward. 'But never another sight of Marshal Brand, the man who really put an end to Jude Lovell?'

Scrapes shrugged. 'That's right. Guess he found that cabin he was always dreaming about. But not hereabouts, that's for sure.'

'And the judge?' asked another man.

'Well, I guess we ain't too anxious to see him again, eh? Judges tend to arrive on the back of bad news.'

Scrapes poured another measure, sampled it and smacked his lips again. 'But, say, if you folks are waitin' on the stage — due by my reckonin' in about an hour — I've got the time to tell you in some detail of how Jude Lovell got here in the first place.'

He shifted the bottle just a fraction as a prompt, and sighed reflectively. 'It was up there, in the Bigbones, when I first saw them bounty hunters leadin' Jude Lovell down the trail to Saracen . . .'

THE END

We do hope that you have enjoyed reading this large print book.

Did you know that all of our titles are available for purchase?

We publish a wide range of high quality large print books including:
Romances, Mysteries, Classics
General Fiction
Non Fiction and Westerns

Special interest titles available in large print are:
The Little Oxford Dictionary
Music Book, Song Book
Hymn Book, Service Book

Also available from us courtesy of Oxford University Press:
Young Readers' Dictionary
(large print edition)
Young Readers' Thesaurus
(large print edition)

For further information or a free brochure, please contact us at:
Ulverscroft Large Print Books Ltd.,
The Green, Bradgate Road, Anstey,
Leicester, LE7 7FU, England.
Tel: (00 44) **0116 236 4325**
Fax: (00 44) **0116 234 0205**

Other titles in the
Linford Western Library:

BOTH SIDES OF THE LAW

Hank J. Kirby

A full hand in draw poker changed Hardin's life — and almost ended it. First there was the shoot-out with the house gambler. Then suspicion of bank robbery, enforced recruitment into a posse, gunfights in the hills and pursuit by both sides of the law in strange country. He'd never had so much trouble! What should he do? Drift on, away from this hellhole, or stay and fight? There was no real choice — it was fight or die . . .

LIZARD WELLS

Caleb Rand

After losing his whole family to a bloodthirsty army patrol, Ben Brooke takes to the desolate Ozark snowline. Years later, he returns to the town called Lizard Wells, where the guilty soldiers have degenerated into guerrillas, bringing brutal disorder to the town. Also living there is the tough Erma Flagg — and more importantly, Moses, a young Cheyenne half-breed . . . After a wild thunderstorm crushes the town, Ben, in desperate need of help, chooses to step single-handedly into a final reckoning.

MISFIT LIL FIGHTS BACK

Chap O'Keefe

Misfit Lil wouldn't allow the rustlers to run off some of her pa's improved Flying G beeves. She started a stampede that trampled them bloodily into the dust. But then two assassins gunned down horse rancher Sundown Sander's son Jimmie. And he had made no move to defend himself, despite Lil's stormy ride to bring him warning. Could devious madam Kitty Malone or gambling-hall owner Flash Sam Whittaker tell the truth about Jimmie's fatal resignation? Lil had to find out.

SHOOT-OUT AT BIG KING

Lee Lejeune

Billy Bandro arrives in Freshwater Creek in Wyoming to start a new life away from riding with the killer outlaw Wesley Toms. When Toms is captured, Billy is assigned to drive him to Laramie for trial, but Toms' gang bushwhack the coach, leave Billy for dead, and take Nancy Partridge and her Aunt Emily hostage. The gambler Slam Beardsley saves Billy, and they ride off in pursuit. But there are many surprises for them in the mountains . . .

ROLLING THUNDER

Owen G. Irons

The town, once a thriving community, was now rotten. Even Tyler Holt, who'd never been browbeaten, lay dead, lynched by a mob. It was all down to Tom Quinn, leader of the first settlers, to return Stratton to its former prosperity. Stratton Valley, with its lush grass, rightfully belonged to him, but what could he do? As he faced the might of Peebles and his cohorts who controlled Stratton, only his courage and gun skills could save the day . . .